BEAVER COATS AND GUNS

The Adventures Of Radisson And Des Groseilliers

RICHARD LAPOINTE

BEAVER COATS AND GUNS

Although the non-native characters presented in this book are mainly based on historical figures, their dialog and many of their actions are invented. By contrast, the indigenous protagonists and their dialog are almost entirely imaginary. Nevertheless, this historical fiction adheres to known facts, while taking liberties where the truth may be open to interpretation.

ISBN-13 978-0991731138

ISBN-10 0991731131

PART ONE

MOHAWK ADVENTURES

Chapter One
Iroquois Ambush

Mohawk Valley, Iroquois Territory – 1652

Outside, it was still dark. In the longhouse where I slept someone near me breathed deeply; farther away, another snored.

Unable to get back to sleep, my thoughts drifted back to the strange journey that brought me here.

It began a few weeks ago, in Trois Rivières, New France, a small settlement and fur trading post on the St. Lawrence River, halfway between Montréal and Québec, where I lived with my sister and two little nephews . . .

When I shut the door to our one-room cabin behind me, Marguérite was still sleeping, the boys snuggled against her. Outside two friends were waiting, and together we strode out the gates of Trois Rivières. It was the first warm day of spring and we were going duck hunting down by the river.

The morning passed by and, even though we didn't shoot many birds, we were enjoying ourselves. Then, Jacques – eighteen, and the oldest – said, "We had better turn back."

"Why so soon," I said. "The day's only half gone and we don't even have enough to make a meal with."

"Because," Jacques said, "if any Iroquois are around they could have heard our guns."

"Then, there's nothing to worry about. Nobody's seen any since last fall; besides, we've got plenty of ammunition."

"You don't know what you are talking about. By the time you got here last fall it was the beginning of winter and they were already gone. I'm telling you, they are giants and they are demons."

"Nonsense. They couldn't be any worse than the toughs I confronted on the streets of Paris. Go back if you want to. I'm staying."

Later, with as many ducks as I could carry I headed back to the fort, passing a pond along the way.

What I found there haunts me to this day.

In the grass by the water my friends lay dead and horribly maimed. Blood everywhere.

Though scared to death I forced myself to look at them.

André, Jacques's younger brother and my best friend, had been shot three times. Twice through the chest, and once between the eyes. Tomahawk blows smashed and dented his skull.

Jacques's torso was punctured all over with knife wounds, and his head was also bashed in.

The tops of their heads were raw and bloody, where both had been scalped. André's terrified eyes stared at the sky, while face down next to him Jacques appeared asleep.

Even though I trembled from head to toe I had to overcome my fear and find out how long they had been dead. Kneeling down, I forced myself to touch their corpses.

Still warm. Their killers can't be far. My heart pounded as I tore myself away. Slowly, I began retracing my steps. Then, hidden among the reeds at the water's edge, I perceived the backs of several enemy heads.

Hoping they hadn't seen me, but determined not to go down without a fight if they had, I rammed a bullet on top of the bird shot already in my gun.

Terrifying shrieks filled the air as a swarm of Iroquois rose up and rushed towards me. Just as they reached me, I fired.

I tried fighting them off but it was futile. Several pinned me to the ground while others took away my weapons; then two of them yanked me to my feet and pulled me along with them through the woods.

A short distance away we came to a clearing where André's and Jacques's scalps hung from a tree. When they made me sit under it I felt faint. While I sat, shivering with fear, they gathered around in a circle to decide – I thought – what to do with me. Realizing escape was impossible, I only hoped they let me live.

To take my mind off my friends' fate, and what mine might also be, I studied the Iroquois closely. All their faces were painted red and they wore nothing but short deerskin skirts. Instead of shoes they had on deerhide moccasins that fit like slippers. Everyone carried a gun, a sword, a knife, and a hatchet. And, hanging by leather cords around their necks, they had ox horn containers to keep their gunpowder dry and leather pouches filled with lead shot.

When their meeting ended they dragged me through the woods again until we came to where they had left their canoes beside the river. As it was almost dark when we arrived, after making me sit down, they hurried about gathering wood for a fire.

By this time I had the impression they planned to take me with them. But what fate awaited me I didn't know. The Iroquois often took prisoners to be their servants but what, I wondered, would they do with a youth belonging to the nation they despised most of all.

After a primitive supper of boiled rancid meat, they made me lie between two of them under a woolen blanket full of holes. Then, praying for the best, I shut my eyes.

Chapter Two
Journey To Anihé

In five canoes, the Iroquois paddled up the St. Lawrence River, heading west along the south side.

As Trois Rivières faded in the distance, and my hopes with it, I rode in the bow of one of their canoes with my hands tied to a thwart in front of me, and with time to think of where I came from and where I was going.

I thought of the grief Andre's and Jacques's family must have suffered when their bodies were found. I, myself, still finding their deaths hard to believe. They had been young and full of life; now gone forever. None of us, family or friends, would ever see them again. Thinking about their being dead filled my heart with sorrow, while remembering how they died and the sight of their bloody scalps hanging from a tree almost paralyzed me with fear.

Would I ever see Marguérite or my two nephews again, I wondered, also feeling badly for having left her alone once more. The reason I came to New France was to help her after the Iroquois killed her husband; now here I was, also taken away from her by the Iroquois.

I remembered my arrival in Québec last fall, a year after Marguérite's letter appealing for my help reached me in France. Then, before continuing to

Trois Rivières where she lived, I stayed on waiting for the start of winter, when the Iroquois would be gone from the St. Lawrence Valley.

To pass the time I made friends with some of the Jesuits living in the seminary near Fort St. Louis which protected Québec from the highest point of Cape Diamond, the promontory overlooking the St. Lawrence River. Around the fort, the officers, administrators, and priests lived – in the area known even then as upper town. The ordinary inhabitants lived down below, in lower town, among the docks and warehouses by the river.

In a small log schoolhouse along the banks of the river, I sat in on classes the Jesuits gave to some of the Algonquin and Huron natives living in the vicinity. While the Jesuits taught them the Gospel in their own tongues I listened in, and soon began to understand and speak both of their languages.

Then at the end of the day the Jesuits would invite me to join them at a tavern by the docks in lower town, where a cheerful blaze in the fireplace kept us warm and the dampness out. It was a popular meeting place for the soldiers and priests who made up a large portion of the capital's five hundred or so inhabitants. Shelter from the cold outside and the tavern's good beer facilitated many an animated conversation.

One of my favorite Jesuits was Father Simon Le Moyne who, though a man of fifty or so, had bright gray eyes and youthful rosy cheeks. Kind and wise, he had an extensive knowledge and understanding of the native peoples and the land. He was also a recognized expert in the languages the Huron and the Iroquois spoke.

As the differences and similarities among the native tongues were puzzling to me, on one of our visits to the tavern in lower town, I asked Father Le Moyne about them. "Although they live close to one another, the languages the Huron and the Algonquin speak are not at all alike," I said. "Can you explain to me why?"

"I'll do my best," Father Le Moyne said. "The Huron speak a variation of the tongue the Iroquois use because, long before we came to this country, they used to live near the Iroquois on the south side of the lake the Iroquois call Ontario – which by the way in their language means 'beautiful lake.' For reasons unknown to us, they crossed to the north side and settled beside another of the Great Lakes, the one we call Lake Huron.

The Huron grew corn and prospered in their new home, with many large villages. We established a mission there, we called Sainte-Marie among the Huron, and for more than twenty years brought them Christ's word. Then the Iroquois came and destroyed their land, killing thousands of Huron and making martyrs of several of our Fathers. The Huron here are the remnants we brought to live under our protection. We took most of them to live on Ile d'Orléans, ten miles downriver from here."

"And what about the Algonquin? They seem to belong to many different nations that speak the same language."

"You are right about the Algonquin. Unlike the Iroquois they are not united into one nation, but are made up of many smaller ones scattered across the country who share a common language and common beliefs. They are important to the fur trade and also, because they believe in a supreme being they call the Great Spirit, the Algonquin are more receptive to Christian instruction than either the Huron or the Iroquois."

"Father, you've said the Iroquois belong to one nation. Can you tell me a little about it?"

"As I understand it, long before our arrival here, there were five separate Iroquois nations – the Mohawk, the Oneida, the Onondaga, the Cayuga and the Seneca. Though all shared a common language they were often at war with one another. Then, according to their legend, a wise Mohawk chief whose name was Hiawatha brought peace and united them into a political union we call the Iroquois Confederacy."

"Where do the Iroquois live?" I asked.

"The Mohawk are the nearest to us, reached by going up a river named after Cardinal Richelieu that flows into the St. Lawrence. The other Iroquois live west of the Mohawk, on the south side of Lake Ontario."

When Father Le Moyne was telling me about the Iroquois I never imagined finding myself one day on the way to their country, tied up as a prisoner. Now, to survive, I knew I would have to overcome my fears and use both my wits and everything the Jesuits taught me about the way the Iroquois thought.

Though bound, I paid attention to their conversations hoping to learn where we were going and what they planned to do with me. Because of its similarity to Huron, from what I could understand of what my abductors said I concluded they were Mohawk and that they were taking me to their land. It was reached by going up the Richelieu River and beyond Lake Champlain – where the French troubles with the Iroquois began forty years before – to the Mohawk Valley, close to the Dutch in New Holland, in what today is the English colony of New York.

As our journey progressed up the Richelieu and across Lake Champlain, my captors began to treat me more kindly, which helped lessen my anxiety. As well, they began to allow me greater liberty – first only untying me at night; then a few days after my capture not tying me at all.

I began to view them differently too. Without their war paint on they didn't seem like the monsters who had attacked me and killed my friends. I saw that they were friendly, laughed often, and liked to amuse themselves by teasing one another and fooling around.

As they got to know me better they befriended me and, as we became better acquainted, wanted me to look like them. When we stopped at night they wanted me to let them comb and grease my hair. Then, after dusting it with red powder and tying it behind my head, they handed me a mirror. When I saw my reflection I laughed, and they laughed with me.

After a week had passed I began to lose my fear of them, dwelling less on the tragedy that befell me and my friends and more on what lay ahead. Having concluded that to survive among them I would need to know their language, I asked them to teach me. I picked it up quickly, while they made sure I pronounced every word properly.

I became friends with their captain, Aweegatay, and began riding in his canoe. At first he did all the paddling while I sat in the bow with nothing to do except look for landmarks along the way in case I managed to escape.

One morning, though, during the second week of our voyage, having passed Lake Champlain and started down a river that flowed south instead of north, he handed me a paddle and said, "Row."

Eagerly, reaching ahead, I dug my paddle deep into the water; then pulled back with all my might, switching from one side to the other with each stroke.

But we hadn't gone far before he spoke again. "Stop. You're not doing it right. Look, all you have to do is dip your paddle a little ways below the surface and pull straight back, like this. Paddle on one side only, and let me take care of the steering."

After we had gone a short distance, me following his example, and seeing we kept up with the others, I said, "How am I doing?"

"Fine, you'll soon be as good as one of us." In the other canoes, everyone laughed.

Another day, coming around a bend in a river we saw a large buck standing beside it. Aweegatay signaled to the others to stop. Then, handing me his gun, he said, "See if you can shoot it from here."

Everyone kept still while I took careful aim. Then too late the buck, sensing our presence, lifted his head, crowned with magnificent antlers. He looked our way, and I fired. The animal fell to the ground, and my companions cheered.

In this agreeable way – heading ever farther south away from Trois Rivières – our journey progressed. Stopping often to hunt, or fish, and ending each day with feasts and songs, enjoying myself so much I sometimes felt I was on a great adventure, almost forgetting I was actually their prisoner and they had murdered my friends.

Then, almost three weeks after leaving Trois Rivières, everything changed. Our pleasant diversions ended when, as we got close to one of their settlements, another war-party joined us leading several Huron prisoners bound and tied together.

The next day we came to the outskirts of Anihé, the Mohawk village where Aweegatay and his companions lived. It was dark when we arrived and the Huron, afraid to enter at night, begged the Mohawk to let us sleep in the woods. They agreed, and from our camp that night we saw light from bonfires in the village a mile away turning the sky as red as hell's inferno.

Early the following morning we were herded towards the village, enclosed within a wall of sharpened poles and surrounded on all sides by fields. I was now tied to the other prisoners and together we walked in a chain across fields where women, preparing the soil for planting, stopped to stare and jeer at us.

Coming closer to the village the excited clamor of voices and the sharp barking of dogs reached our ears, growing louder and more frenzied with each step we took.

About a quarter of a mile from the entrance, our guards made us sit down. In front of us, extending all the way to the village gates, two rows of men, women, and children formed a corridor. Armed with sticks and other instruments of torture they glowered at us from the gauntlet our captors said we all must run through.

"Take off your clothes," one of the guards with the Huron said to me, "and prepare to run as fast as you can. If you make it to the other end without falling your life will be spared."

Staring down the corridor of menacing faces, my heart beat so fast I thought it would burst. Vainly, I looked around for Aweegatay. But he was nowhere in sight.

Then, just as I prepared to run for my life, he stepped out of the crowd. An older woman, who was with him, covered my nakedness with a blanket; then, with his hatchet in one hand and my hand in the other, he led me through the threatening mob. No one tried to stop us.

Aweegatay and the woman, who in fact was his mother, took me to a bark-covered dwelling where they offered me food, although I was still too afraid to eat.

Then they left me there alone. While they were gone some of the neighbors peered through the doorway.

A group of old men wearing blankets arrived and sat across from me puffing silently on their pipes. After awhile they made me go with them to a larger building where more white haired men, also smoking, sat around a fire.

"Sit here, by the fire," one of them said, which made me afraid they meant to burn me alive.

The arrival of Aweegatay's mother lifted my spirits. Standing in front of the circle of elders she addressed them in a clear and forceful voice.

"The young Frenchman is brave and strong," she said. "When my son and the others attacked him he didn't run, but stood his ground the way a warrior facing death should.

"Aweegatay and his friends told me he is a good hunter and on the journey here worked as hard as them. They say he's been learning our language and ways too.

"Surely, then, this can only be the work of the Great Spirit who has sent him among us in place of my son who died in the war with the French one year ago."

The elders having listened attentively signaled their agreement with what she said with a chorus of, "ho, ho's."

Having gained the elders' approval, Aweegatay's mother removed a cloth sash from around her waist and after tying it around mine led me out of the council house.

On the way to her dwelling I heard the distant screams and wailing of women from the place where fires of hell burned and prisoners were tortured. Instinctively, I gripped Aweegatay's mother's hand tighter.

By the time we got back it was dark. After giving me a little supper she showed me to my bed and covered me with furs.

Chapter Three
My Mohawk Family

When daylight began seeping in, I sat up and looked around.

The longhouse was rectangular, maybe thirty feet long by twenty wide, and covered with large sheets of bark attached to a framework of poles. In the shadows beneath an arched roof I made out ears of corn and tobacco sheaves hanging from rafters.

The platform where I slept was about two feet off the ground and half the length of the longhouse, with another one along the opposite wall. Here and there, covered with animal skins, I distinguished the shapes of others, sleeping. Shelves above our beds held clay pots, baskets, blankets, snowshoes, and other household items.

Next to a front entrance several large bark containers sat on the ground, and near them a mortar made from a hollowed out tree trunk with a wooden pestle, almost as tall as a man. From the corn husk leaves and threshed cobs on the dirt floor around it, I guessed it was used to grind corn into flour.

Just then, Aweegatay's mother carrying a bundle of sticks came in through a deerhide curtain covering the entrance.

I watched her put the bundle down next to a fire pit near the door; then arrange dried grass and twigs over smoldering coals, and kneel close and blow on them. When a small yellow flame leaped to life she added bigger pieces, and soon a fire crackled, sending light into every corner and wisps of white smoke through an opening in the roof.

When it burned to her satisfaction she got up and filled a wooden bowl with corn flour from one of the bark vessels by the door. To the flour she added water from a clay pot, grease from a leather pouch and dried berries from another container.

Having all the ingredients she needed she sat down by the fire and began mixing everything together with a wooden spoon. Feeling hungry, I got up.

"Good morning . . . did you sleep well," Aweegatay's mother said as I sat down near her.

I was surprised to hear her address me in the Huron tongue, which I had learned in Québec. I supposed Aweegatay had told her I knew it. Answering in the same language, I said, "Yes I did, after you saved my life."

"You deserved it. Now you must be hungry . . . well, don't worry I'll soon have something for you."

Then, as I watched her ladle cornmeal batter onto a cedar plank, she said, "It wasn't really I who saved you. It was the Great Spirit who brought you here, and because of that we must take good care of you."

As she set her tray of biscuits among some ashes the fire illuminated her copper toned face, accenting fine lines around her mouth and eyes and threads of silver in her long black hair.

When the cakes were arranged to her satisfaction, she spoke again in her gentle way. "Your father's name is Sagoyewatha. He is a great warrior and hunter who's equally renowned for his oratory," she said. After pausing to push hot coals closer to the biscuits, she continued. "In my time, I have had nine children. Five died very young, and last year in the war with the French I lost a son who was very dear to me. Now all I have left are Aweegatay and my two daughters . . . ah, here comes Conharrasan now."

Conharrasan, rubbing the sleep from her eyes, smiled at me and said, "I'm glad you've come to live with us . . . it will be fun having a boy my own age to do things with."

"It's kind of you to say so. I also look forward to spending time together," I said in the halting Iroquois I was still learning. Though awkwardly expressed, I meant every word, for the sight of her almost made me forget where I came from. She was pretty with a lovely figure, outlining the soft deerhide dress she wore that came down to her knees.

Before we could talk more her mother said, "Conharrasan, we need water."

"Come with me," she said.

"Where do you get it," I said when we were outside.

"From the river beside the village."

Walking along the straight and narrow streets we met other early risers. And everyone – among them, I'm sure, some who would gladly have beat me yesterday – greeted us warmly.

Though here the streets were flanked with bark covered lodges instead of log cabins, I was reminded of Trois Rivières; however, Anihé then had considerably more than my village's less than one hundred families.

At the river Conharrasan waded in up to her knees. After filling the clay pot she brought with her, she joined me on the grassy bank where I waited.

For a while we sat without speaking, listening to the gurgling stream. In the warm sun, water drops glistened on her smooth brown arms and legs.

"What's your mother's name," I said, breaking the silence.

"Gannendaris."

"She is very kind."

"Yes she is, and wise too. When she was my age my grandfather's army took her from the Huron.

Now, though born a Huron, she has much influence among our people."

"She must have been beautiful when she was young."

"My father says she was the prettiest girl in the village."

"As you are now."

With a pleased smile, Conharrasan then asked, "How old are you?"

"Sixteen, and you?"

"This is my fifteenth spring. Gannendaris says these are the best years of our lives. Don't you think so too?"

But before I could answer she said, "We had better head back."

Inside the lodge the sweet aroma of Gannendaris' cornmeal biscuits filled the air.

Everyone helped themselves to biscuits and pieces of smoked fish, and while the others were busy eating I glanced around at my adopted family.

There was Sagoyewatha, the patriarch who though nearly sixty years old was very fit. Like medals earned in past battles he wore a multitude of scars on his weathered skin.

Aweegatay, who I got to know well on the long journey to Anihé, was muscular and tall. A worthy representative, I thought, of the Iroquois race known for its physical strength and intelligence.

The name of the youngest was Gahano. A year younger than Conharrasan she was pretty and almost as tall, though slimmer.

When our appetites were satisfied we drank an infusion made from a mixture of dried roots steeped in hot water.

Then, while we sat enjoying our tea, Sagoyewatha made himself comfortable on a bearskin rug spread out before the hearth. After lighting a long-stemmed clay pipe and puffing on it for awhile – in apparent contemplation – he spoke.

"Now that the young Frenchman is going to live with us he'll need to conduct himself like a Mohawk," he said.

"If he is to be one of us, he'll need new clothes," Gannendaris said.

"Of course, for the honor of the family he must be properly dressed."

"I'm sure the girls will give me a hand."

"I'll be glad to help," Conharrasan said.

"Me too. I can sew, you know," Gahano said.

"Until he has some of his own, he can take one of my Dutch shirts; then, later, when he's ready, I'll introduce him to my friends," Aweegatay said.

"Very good, but no man can be a Mohawk without a gun." Having said this Sagoyewatha reached up into the rafters and retrieved a wooden box, which he handed to me.

"Open it," he said.

Inside there was a gleaming new Dutch pistol. After examining it carefully I said, "Thank you. This is the best gun I have ever owned. I'll use it to get fresh meat for Gannendaris' sagamité," meaning the stew the Iroquois made, starting from a base of corn flour.

"Well spoken, my son," Sagoyewatha said. "Use this one for shooting small animals and birds. Then later, when you are ready, you shall have a gun powerful enough to kill bears and deer with, as well as our enemies."

Then Sagoyewatha and Aweegatay went out, leaving me alone with Gannendaris and her daughters.

Immediately they set about the task of making me a new suit of clothes. Gannendaris cut out rectangular pieces of deerhide which Conharrasan and Gahano helped her sew into a pair of leggings reaching to my thighs. For adornment they finished the seams with fringes of leather strips.

Next, Gannendaris made a breechcloth from a long piece of hide about a foot in width, which she showed me how to wrap around my waist so the ends hung between my legs, in front and behind.

When I was attired in my new outfit Conharrasan and Gahano combed and arranged my hair while I serenaded them with French songs, which made them burst into fits of giggles.

Before long they judged me ready to go out in public. Outside I enjoyed the soft feel of my new deerskin pants and moccasins decorated with dyed porcupine quills. Wearing the clean white linen shirt Aweegatay gave me, and with my hair freshly combed and greased, Conharrasan and Gahano took me around the village, showing me off to the friendly inhabitants who came out to see me.

I soon became accustomed to life among the Mohawk. The youths of Anihé accepted me as one of them, and invited me to take part in their daily pastimes. Sometimes we went on hunting excursions, from which I always brought back small game – squirrels and partridges, and the like – which I gave to Gannendaris. On other days we'd compare our strength and skills in wrestling, running, or tomahawk throwing contests. I excelled in all their sports, which earned me their respect and admiration.

Besides these agreeable pastimes there were many other aspects of life among the Mohawk that appealed to me. I admired their camaraderie, generosity, and cooperative spirit. But what I found most attractive about my life here was a feeling of freedom and independence – of being able to do whatever I pleased.

There were no laws or moral prohibitions to constrain us. No Governor ruled over our village, and no Jesuit priest scolded us for our conduct. Yet the Mohawk lived in greater harmony than the French. Here, in the wilderness of the New World, far from the capitals of Europe, I discovered an atmosphere of equality and freedom perfectly suited to my own free spirit.

While I roamed the Mohawk Valley freely, the inhabitants of New England, New Holland, and New France clung to fortified settlements along the Atlantic coast and the St. Lawrence River, unable to survive without the food and supplies carried every summer on ships from Europe. And without someone to guide them, they dared not enter the dark forest outside.

And while Europeans remained trapped inside their forts, the natives of the New World travelled great distances in vessels made from tree bark. Wherever there were rivers and lakes, their canoes carried them. Along the way, thousands of lakes and streams nourished them with fish while the woods provided them with meat. They, alone, were able to survive without help in this rugged land. And, generously, they shared their secrets with trusted newcomers like me.

But it was the warmth and kindness of my adopted family that contributed most to my contentment. Gannendaris, whom I called mother, was unceasing in her attentions to my well-being. Conharrasan and Gahano, now my sisters, enlivened the household with their irrepressible spirits. From Aweegatay I learned how to read the land, and from Sagoyewatha the history and traditions of his people.

As weeks went by and I got to know their language better, Sagoyewatha began to give me a better understanding of why the Iroquois went to war so much. Our conversations often took place in the evenings, sitting outside by a fire while Sagoyewatha smoked his pipe.

"Why are the Iroquois at war with the Algonquin and the French?" I asked him one warm night.

"To understand our reasons we must go back to my great grandfather's time," he said, "when some of our people were living in Stadacona, in the place your big chief lives today. One day, ships with Frenchmen arrived. They got caught in the ice and had to spend the winter in Stadacona. Without proper nourishment their gums turned black and began to bleed, and they would have died if our forefathers had not made tea from spruce trees for them."

Sagoyewatha was talking about Jacques Cartier

and his men who more than a century ago spent the winter in what is now Québec, where they suffered from scurvy. Sagoyewatha continued, "Each year the French came to fish and trade their goods for our furs. It was a fair exchange, and for a while we were friends with the French. Then the Algonquin from farther downriver, who also traded with the French and were more numerous in those parts than ourselves, forced us to return to our valley here. Many years later, when the French returned to live in Stadaconna they sided with the Algonquin in their war with us, and now we are at war with both."

"But the Huron and other nations, such as the Erie west of here, why do you go to war with them?" I asked. It was a question to which even the Jesuits were not sure of the answer.

"After the Algonquin took the fur trade with the French away from us, we traded with the Dutch when they built a settlement near us. Then the beaver, whose pelts the white man wants most, began to disappear from our land. And when we tried to get them from the Huron who used to trade with nations farther north they wouldn't give them to us because they had a flourishing trade with the French. Then the Dutch gave us guns which we used to destroy the Huron and take over the trade."

"What about the Erie?"

"The Erie and other nations like them, including

the Huron, are related to us," Sagoyewatha said. "Their languages are similar. We go to war with them to expand our army and to strengthen our union. We do it to make them join us, to be stronger together, and to let them enjoy the freedom and security that comes with belonging to the Iroquois Confederacy."

"But why does the Confederacy need to expand?" I asked, still failing to see the reason for it.

"Every year more white men arrive to occupy our land. First it was the French, then the Dutch, and now another people they call the English, who have begun to expand west. To stop them we – the Iroquois – must become even stronger, take back our land and add more of the nations who share our language to the Confederacy," Sagoyewatha said.

"Across the sea, the village I lived in was more than a hundred times bigger than Anihé, and there are many more villages just as big. There is not enough land for everyone, so more will certainly come," I said.

"Now you see why we are anxious to conquer all our enemies," Sagoyewatha said.

Chapter Four
A Mother's Love

With the passing of spring and the arrival of summer I came to think of Gannendaris as both my mother and my best friend. Her love and kindness helped me to feel at ease in a strange and unfamiliar land. Whenever I needed comfort or advice I turned to her.

Partly she loved me because of her belief the Great Spirit sent me in place of the son she lost in the war with the French. As for myself, I admired her as much for her generosity as for her wisdom. To me she represented all that was good in the Iroquois.

Often, usually late morning or early afternoon, I would slip away from one of my companions' frequent contests and seek her out. In good weather she might be outside, perhaps scraping the fat and flesh from a deerhide, or inside if it rained, performing some other domestic chore such as making or mending clothes. Quietly I would sit down beside her and she would look up and smile, her busy fingers never stopping their work.

Little by little, I learned the details of her life. Long ago, when a young Huron, the Mohawk captured and brought her to Anihé where she met Sagoyewatha, who found her to his liking. Their marriage was a happy one and they had many children together.

One warm afternoon during one of these encounters she said, "It would please me very much if you would become more familiar with my daughters."

Noticing my astonishment, she went on, "Among our people it is customary for young women to sleep with more than one man before settling down for life. In this way they are better prepared to find suitable lifelong companions."

"Where I come from our priests don't allow men and women to sleep together before they are married. Also, because there are fewer women than men, by the time girls reach Conharrasan's or even Gahano's age most are already married," I said.

"I remember your Black Robes from my youth. They told us the same thing. They said it was bad the way our young women made love whenever they wanted to. They said their God didn't like it. Apparently, though, some of the young men who came with them didn't think our customs so bad. In fact, they were so eager to adopt our ways their conduct with our young women scandalized the elders, who were normally tolerant of such matters." Gannendaris chuckled at the recollection of this old and favorite anecdote.

Becoming serious again, she returned to the subject uppermost in her mind. "You know I love you like my own son, and I love my daughters dearly," she said. "For this reason, and because I want my girls to enjoy their youth, which will pass by all too quickly, I want you to take pleasure in them. They love you very much, you know, as we all do."

Listening to this extraordinary request I felt the color rise in my cheeks. Nevertheless, ignoring my embarrassment, she continued.

"Conharrasan has already had a lover, but Gahano hasn't. It would make me happy if you would make love to her. She's told me she wants you to be the first."

Chapter Five
A Happy Longhouse

Following my unusual conversation with Gannendaris, I began to look at my Mohawk sisters differently. Until then I never thought of them as anything other than amusing and gentle companions.

To tell the truth I didn't have much experience with girls. In Trois Rivières, where the Jesuits and their parents kept a close eye on them, boys like me took pleasure in other pursuits such as hunting and drinking beer.

Neither, before, had the absence of female company been much of a hardship. After all, I was just a youth, my head filled with thoughts of adventure. But now that Gannendaris had aroused my interest I thought of little else.

One evening, a few days later, Conharrasan said, "Near here there is a meadow full of strawberries. In the morning Gahano and I are going to pick some. Would you like to come?"

"I would love to. I've heard the ones here taste better than the colorless fruit of my native land."

"Good, then tonight I'll sleep next to you. This way we can leave early without disturbing the others."

That night when Conharrasan took her place

beneath the covers the heat of her body close to mine made me want to reach out and touch her. But, not knowing what to do next if I did, I pretended to be sleepy. Feigning a yawn, I said, "Goodnight Conharrasan."

"Goodnight, handsome brother. Sweet dreams."

The next morning we followed a trail through the woods, filled with the sounds of birds singing and leaves fluttering. I walked behind Conharrasan and Gahano who skipped along, reed baskets balanced on their heads.

Before long we came to a clearing beside a stream. "This is the place," Conharrasan said, stopping to pick a few small red berries for me to try.

"Hmm, sweet and juicy."

"Well, let's hurry and fill our baskets. Afterwards we can take it easy and enjoy ourselves before we have to go back."

Together we spread out in the meadow searching for the bright red fruit hidden in long grass still wet with morning dew. Around us birds darted about, butterflies floated and bees hovered from flower to flower, while the sun grew hotter in a clear blue sky.

When I had filled a small bark container I went over to empty it into one of the larger ones

Conharrasan brought. She smiled as I approached – her strawberry stained lips inviting.

I reached for her hand, and she took it. "You are beautiful," I said, pulling her closer. But before I could put an arm around her waist she pulled free and ran across the meadow.

I caught up to her near the edge of the woods, and when I took her in my arms she laughed, until I silenced her with a kiss. She didn't resist and pressed her mouth against mine, her breath warm and sweet.

Then she pulled me to the ground where I lay on my back while she ran a hand underneath my shirt. Soon she made me sit up to take it off. Then, as she was unraveling my breechcloth and pulling off my leggings, she kissed my chest and neck everywhere. Finally, when I was completely undressed, she removed her deerhide shift and lay naked beside me.

"Let me look at you," I said.

Lying before me she allowed me time to enjoy her beauty. Gently, I began exploring her body with my hands. Skin smooth as silk, breasts wonderful to touch.

While I kissed her moist lips she took one hand and guided it across her flat stomach to the silky crest of black hair below. She directed my fingers down and with a sigh opened her legs. Then she took hold of me and pulled me into her. And, with Conharrasan and instinct my guides, I made love for the first time.

Lying together in the grass afterwards, she told me she loved me.

"You aren't like other boys," she said. "You like to sing and talk to me, and you spend almost as much time with me as with your friends. Many of the boys here are rough, not interested in anything except hunting and sports. When they do talk they want to boast about what good hunters they are or what great warriors they are going to be. Since you've come to live with us, they don't interest me anymore.

"I like your looks, too," she said. "Your hair is long and straight, and shiny dark brown like beaver fur. Your nose is manly, your chin bold, and your cheekbones high. With your skin dark from the sun you look like one of us. And I love your light brown eyes and your beautiful mouth. Here, let me kiss you."

Not finished yet, she found more about me she liked. Moving her hands over my body, she said, "You have wonderful broad shoulders and smooth muscular arms, and a firm chest and small waist, too. And I love your strong and shapely legs . . . and this. Oh, look how big it grows."

The next day on our way to gather more

strawberries I walked hand in hand with Conharrasan. Whenever we stopped to kiss along the way Gahano would stand behind us, arms folded, one foot tapping until we moved on.

At the meadow, barely able to keep our hands off one another, we raced to the same secluded place we made love the day before. Gahano followed.

When Conharrasan had found a place for us on the grass she said, "Come lie down beside me."

"I can't, not with Gahano watching."

Conharrasan got up and went with Gahano until they were out of hearing. After they spoke awhile Gahano left.

Again we made love in the fertile field, and it was better than the first time.

Afterwards, as we lay side by side looking up at the sky, Conharrasan said, "Gahano is unhappy."

"Why?"

"Because she wants you to be her lover as well."

"But I'm happy with just you."

"And I'm happy with you but we mustn't be selfish. We need to think about the happiness of others, like Gahano and Gannendaris."

"What does Gannendaris have to do with it?"

"You know that Gahano is a virgin and

Gannendaris wants you to be her first lover. It's important to her. If you don't want to do it for Gahano, think of our mother."

"But what about you, won't you be jealous?"

"I want you to be happy. That's what's most important to me. But I also want my sister and my mother to be happy. I'll be happy if you make love to Gahano because then she'll be happy, and Gannendaris will be happy, and you'll be happy, too. Don't you see? It's the best way to make everyone happy."

"But I don't want to lose you," I said.

"Don't worry. You'll have us both. It will be better, you'll see. Now go to her."

Gahano was sitting by the stream on the other side of the meadow. When I sat down beside her she didn't look up, continuing to gaze into the transparent water swirling around her feet.

"What's wrong," I said, seeing tears trickling down her velvety cheeks.

Throwing her arms around me she buried her face against my chest and began to sob. Letting go at last she had a pained expression, and when she managed to speak she sniffled and her chin trembled.

"Am I not a woman too, like Conharrasan?"

"Of course you're becoming one, just like her."

"You don't believe me . . . I can tell. Here, touch me and you will see I am as much a woman as she is."

When I didn't move Gahano placed my hands on her chest. With her hands over mine I felt her breasts. They were small and firm. She moved my fingers to her nipples, which began to swell, and when she let go I continued caressing them, and her breasts.

With a pleased smile she moved her face to mine and began to cover me with soft kisses. As her kisses grew bolder I tingled all over. When the torrent of kisses ceased, I opened my eyes as though emerging from a delicious dream.

"Well," she said.

"Yes Gahano, you're certainly a woman."

"Do you want me," she said softly in my ear.

"Yes . . . I want you."

Conharrasan arrived afterwards with baskets full of strawberries. She smiled and lay down with us. For a while we slept naked in the sun, Conharrasan and Gahano on either side of me. When the afternoon light began to soften, we refreshed ourselves in the stream, where the two of them bathed me. Afterwards they fed me strawberries and combed my hair.

Throughout the strawberry season we returned to the meadow daily. And when they were gone we picked raspberries and blackberries. Each day we exchanged presents – little things like necklaces and bracelets, tinkling bells, combs, and mirrors, or unusual stones and flowers.

At night we slept side by side, the longhouse happy now and Gannendaris content.

Chapter Six
Mohawk Adoption Ceremony

At first, even as with each passing day I lived more and more like a Mohawk, I used to think of the past often. Missing and wondering what had become of the relatives and friends I left behind. But, with the passage of time I thought about them less and less.

Then one day – already late summer, three or four months after my abduction – I woke up feeling troubled and confused. The malaise stayed with me throughout the morning, when I didn't join my friends as usual. Instead, I sat quietly outside our lodge cleaning my pistol, and thinking, while Gannendaris nearby worked on a new pair of moccasins for me.

Am I Mohawk or am I French, I asked myself, over and over again.

On the one hand I missed my family and friends in Trois Rivières and when I thought I might never see Marguérite and my little nephews again, tears came to my eyes.

Yet, I couldn't imagine a kinder household than my present one, nor friends truer than those I had here in Anihé. Gannendaris and Sagoyewatha loved me like a son, while Aweegatay was a devoted brother and a good friend. Then there were Conharrasan and Gahano who loved me dearly and took care of all my needs.

Also, as a Mohawk I enjoyed far greater freedom than most Frenchmen ever could.

Finally, I made up my mind.

Gannendaris looked up from her work and, as though having read my mind, said, "Do you still feel French?" She spoke in the Huron tongue which we often used when I first arrived in Anihé and then understood better than Iroquois.

I frowned and pretended not to understand what she said. Smiling she asked again – this time in Iroquois. "In your heart, are you still a Frenchman?"

"No," I said. "I am Mohawk."

Tears began rolling down her cheeks. "Ovinha," she said, over and over. It was the name of her deceased son and in Gannendaris' mind I embodied his spirit, which in this way the Great Spirit had returned him to her.

Then getting up from her work she said, "I must go find your father and tell him the good news."

When they returned together Sagoyewatha said, "My son, you have brought great joy to your mother's heart and you make me proud. To celebrate and welcome you into our family and our nation, I have called for a banquet in your honor this very day."

With no time to lose, the entire household went to work getting me ready for the ceremony. Conharrasan bathed me, while Gahano combed and greased my hair.

When I was cleaned up Gannendaris gave me a new red blanket to wrap myself in and a red and blue cloth cap. Around my neck she hung two necklaces made of wampum, the small white or mauve seashells that were their most valued treasures.

Conharrasan and Gahano tied more strings of wampum around my neck and wrists, while Aweegatay painted my face red and tied eagle feathers in my hair.

When the others had finished, Sagoyewatha inspected their work.

"I don't like the cap," he said. "It's out of place." After replacing it with a garland of scented flowers, he hung another necklace – so long it almost touched the ground – around my neck. Finally, he thrust a hatchet in my hand.

"Now you are ready," he said.

Then, adorned like a prince and barely able to move, I accompanied my family to the longhouse where the banquet and adoption ceremony were to take place.

More than a hundred guests waited with wooden bowls and spoons for the sagamité bubbling in large iron kettles over fires outside. The Iroquois prepared their sagamité from a base of corn flour mixed with water and bear grease to which they added pieces of meat or fish, and sometimes flowers and berries.

According to etiquette our guests could not eat until Sagoyewatha had spoken. Living up to his nickname, which meant "Keeper Awake," he spoke for a long time.

He began with praise for the Mohawk nation, saying how great and feared it was. Then, he recalled every battle and the names of the famous warriors who fought in them, recalling each one's accomplishments and sacrifices.

At last he began a tribute to his deceased son, Ovinha, whose name I was henceforth to bear.

"Oh, our son. Alas, he is dead. Gone, never to return He died on the battlefield without a friend. With no one to mourn his sad fate. No sister's tears were there. He fell in his prime, when we needed him most to keep us safe. Alas, he is gone, leaving us in sorrow, his loss to cry for.

"How well we remember his deeds. The deer he could take on the chase, the bears that cowered at the sight of his strength. And the enemies who fell at his feet. Brave and courageous in war, he was as harmless as a fawn to those he loved.

"But why do we grieve for his loss? Though he fell in battle, he died a hero, and his spirit went up to the land of his forefathers in war. They received him with joy, and fed him, and clothed him.

"No my friends, he is happy. So dry your tears. His spirit has seen our distress and sent us a helper whom we greet with pleasure. Ovinha has returned. Let us receive him with joy. He is handsome and pleasant. Our son reborn. Gladly do we welcome him here. In place of the one who is dead he will stand. May he always be happy until his spirit must leave us too."

To mark the end of the speech and the start of the banquet Sagoyewatha broke a clay pot of sagamité with his hatchet. Then the gathering sang as everyone held out their bowl for the young boys who served.

When the banquet was finished I stood by the door with my family. As the guests left many stopped to wish me well. Among them, one of the elders who granted my mother custody of me the day I arrived.

"Now you are truly one of us. Welcome, and may you always be happy here," he said.

Chapter Seven
War Fever

The last days of summer faded away. Cold rains and strong north winds followed, and when the sun returned the leaves had turned red and gold. For a brief period, after autumn arrived, the days were warm again, the nights clear and crisp. With the return of good weather I resumed my favorite pastime – hunting small game in the withered fields and rustling woods of the Mohawk Valley.

I was content. Gannendaris made new clothes whenever I needed them, my sisters – now also my lovers – kept me warm at night, and once a month Sagoyewatha gave me a new white shirt he got from the Dutch at Fort Orange. However, although only two days away, he never let me go there with him.

As the days grew shorter, the women got ready for winter. Taking their daughters with them they went into the fields to pick vegetables, then stored dried corn in bark barrels and buried most of the beans and squash in the ground. After the crops were in they went into the woods to gather chestnuts, walnuts, and hazelnuts, as well as plums, cranberries and other fruit they dried and put away for winter.

Then, when only a few dried leaves clung to the trees and the moon rose red and full over fields of pumpkin and wilting corn stalks, the Mohawk celebrated harvest's end with feasts and prayers.

They celebrated the bounty of the season, and thanked the Great Spirit for the corn that kept starvation from their cabins throughout long winter months. And when snow began to fall and cold winds howled they moved inside and listened to the elders tell tales of their youth.

But for warrior-chiefs, like my father, winter was the time to plan campaigns for the following spring. Daily, there were military banquets where warriors danced and whooped, letting out savage cries, and calling for the death of their enemies everywhere.

Sagoyewatha raised his hatchet against the Algonquin nations, the ancient enemies of the Iroquois who lived alongside the French, vowing to annihilate them just as they had destroyed the Huron before. Every night he exhorted young men to go with him to take revenge upon the Algonquin and the French.

"When I was young," he said at a banquet I attended, "my father went to a large lake north of here. They went to confront the Algonquin, who arrived with white men they had never seen before. Our two armies faced one another beside this lake, both armed with spears and bows and arrows while the white men, whose captain wore a metal crown and metal vest, carried guns with long barrels. Before a single arrow was shot or spear thrown, the French, as these white men were, killed our fathers with what to them appeared to be sticks that killed at a distance."

I, of course, knew he was talking about Champlain and his small band of men who joined the Algonquin in their war against the Iroquois almost forty years before, a choice many French regret to this day.

Sagoyewatha continued, "Now armed with Dutch guns, we avenge our fathers' deaths, killing the French and taking the furs they get from the Algonquin nations to buy even more guns with which to drive the French from this land."

Now myself a Mohawk, I wished for nothing more than to join the wars. But worried my father might oppose my wishes I waited for the right moment to gain his approval.

My chance came at a military banquet I attended with my brother. Flushed with pride Sagoyewatha had just finished telling the gathering of young men that Aweegatay would soon be leaving to fight the Erie, their enemy to the west.

"Some may wonder at the father who goes in one direction while leaving his son to go in the other. But do not condemn him for not taking his son on the same warpath as he. For the quickest way to make the world tremble and to have liberty everywhere is to conquer all of our enemies."

"And what am I?" I asked. The room was hushed as everyone waited for Sagoyewatha to reply.

"Why, you are Mohawk like me," he said, presently.

"Then," I said, "let me go with Aweegatay. He is my brother and I love him. If he should die on the warpath I want to die with him."

"Have courage son Ovinha," Sagoyewatha said. "Your namesake died in the wars, not in the cabin. I go to avenge his death. If I die, avenge mine."

I left the banquet encouraged, sure Sagoyewatha would give in eventually and let me go with Aweegatay. However Gannendaris, having lost one son in battle, would not be so easily persuaded.

"You're too young," she said when I consulted her. "You don't know the country, and you'll get lost in the woods. Wait until next year when you are older and better prepared. For now, stay here with your mother and your sisters who love you."

But I was determined to go, and sought the opinion of some of our warriors who had been in the west country where the Erie lived.

"You mustn't miss it," Ahareehon, the captain of the war party against the Erie, said. "It's a beautiful country and easy to cross. And there are all the deer and wild turkey you could want, and Erie as plentiful and easy to kill as turkeys."

I returned to my mother prepared with new arguments to win her over.

"I won't get lost," I said. "The land is flat and

you can see for miles. Neither will I be killed, because they have no guns. And I'll bring back presents for Conharrasan and Gahano and a servant to help you with your work."

But the final say rested with Sagoyewatha, who at last gave his consent.

He made the announcement at a banquet for all the captains who would soon be leaving for the wars. Many came, for Sagoyewatha was a renowned warrior-chief. When the captains in attendance had finished eating, he rose to speak.

"I must tell you I'm sorry to be taking up the hatchet against the Algonquin and the French," he said. Then, after pausing and leaving his guests to wonder what could possibly make such a fearless leader have compassion for an enemy, he said, "It's because it's so damned cold in their country, and for that reason I'm forced to wait to march upon them." The young commanders laughed.

Sagoyewatha went on to say he was willing enough to have his sons leave before him and that the present banquet was in their honor. He told them his adopted son was ready to go with his own to avenge the death of their brother who died in battle two summers before, and he asked our captain, Ahareehon, to look out for us.

The next day Sagoyewatha gave me the gun he promised the day he gave me my Dutch pistol.

"Use it well," he said. "And come back safe. You are very dear to us, my son."

On the night before our departure, Ahareehon invited my brother and me, along with the rest of our troops, to another military banquet. There were ten of us, all young and strong. Though only twenty years of age Ahareehon was already renowned for his boldness and bravery, while Aweegatay had been to the wars twice before. The others were equally experienced. Being the youngest, I was proud to be in the company of such courageous young men.

After eating and singing late into the night, we left Anihé the next morning.

Many of our friends and family members accompanied us to the beginning of the trail that led to the upper country west of us, where the upper Iroquois – the Oneida, the Onondaga, the Cayuga, and the Seneca – lived. When it came time to say goodbye, Conharrasan and Gahano could not hide their tears.

"I'll miss you," Gahano said, while I held her in my arms.

"I'll miss you too."

"Be brave," Conharrasan said as we embraced, "and be careful. I couldn't bear it if anything were to happen to you."

"Don't worry. Nothing will."

Then, after taking one last look at our loved ones, we turned and entered the snow-filled forest.

Chapter Eight
On The Warpath

It was near the end of February when we left. "To reach Erie country before the snow melts, we'll have to hurry," Ahareehon said, as we tramped through the woods.

As well as a gun, a hatchet and a knife, each of us carried a pack with supplies and ammunition. The snowshoes we had strapped to our feet kept us from sinking in the snow, still knee deep in the forest.

I first used them the winter after my arrival in Canada, on my way to Trois Rivières from Québec. Almost as long as a man is tall, and made from a mesh of rawhide stretched over an oval frame of birch wood, they – and the toboggans the Algonquin who accompanied me had – were one of the marvels of the New World that first enthralled me.

After heading northwest for seven days we arrived at the first settlement in what we from the Mohawk Valley in "the lower country" called "the upper country." This village belonged to the Oneida, the smallest of the five nations in the Iroquois Confederacy. We stayed with them two days to rest and mend our equipment, and when we resumed our journey an Oneida youth came with us.

Continuing westward, we arrived the same afternoon in the land of the Onondaga, who often joined the Mohawk in the war against the Algonquin and the French.

Being best friends of the Mohawk, the Onondaga took good care of us. Every day they invited us to several banquets where they gave us the best of what they had – large helpings of venison, corn, and bear meat served in thickened corn flour as well as smoked eel, which was their greatest delicacy. When we left, four days later, they gave us Huron servants to carry our baggage.

After leaving the Onondaga village where we stayed, it took another three days to reach the home of the Cayuga, who like the Oneida were a small nation. The next day, after a short march, we entered the first village of the Seneca, the last of the upper Iroquois and the most populous nation in the Confederacy. Although we had little trouble understanding them I was surprised to learn they spoke a different dialect than the rest of the Iroquois.

After resting two days we left our servants behind and continued westward. Along the way we crossed several large fields, some as much as seven miles across.

I asked Ahareehon about them. "How did such large open spaces as these come to be uninhabited?"

"Seneca lived here until their corn would no

longer grow," he said. "For the same reason all our people move their villages every nine or ten years." Now the only residents of these empty meadows were deer pawing the snow in search of last year's grass.

Still heading west, we passed three more Seneca towns. But, because the snow was beginning to melt, we hurried through, only stopping long enough to eat and rest. As we marched past, the inhabitants pointed at me, amazed to see a white man in a company of Mohawk on the warpath.

A high limestone escarpment marked the end of Iroquois controlled land. "North of here there is a powerful waterfall we call Niagara," Ahareehon said. "It is a wonder to behold, but too far away for us to take the time to visit it. Sometimes, when there is a north wind, it's thunder can be heard from here."

Finally, after climbing the escarpment's steep sides, we came to the edge of a river Ahareehon said would take us to a big lake near to where the Erie lived. Planning to rest and make canoes for the next leg of the journey, we set up camp. We stayed almost ten days, working on the canoes and hunting during the day; then at night, around blazing fires, we gorged ourselves on meat from the deer and wild turkey that abounded in the surrounding woods.

All the materials we needed to make canoes

were close at hand. Using the hatchets and knives we carried for war, we cut down branches and made poles we planted in the ground, forming an outline of the topsides. Next, we removed large sheets of bark from elm trees and, after soaking them in water to make them supple, laid them lengthways along the sides and over the one we laid on bottom, which we covered with cedar planks for a floor. Then, we sewed the bark pieces together with spruce roots, which we also lashed around ash wood thwarts and gunwales, fastened to cedar ribs with wooden pegs. When the structure was finished, we sealed and waterproofed the seams and joints with spruce gum.

When our four canoes – each big enough to hold five men and our baggage – were ready we started down the river. Two days later we entered Lake Erie.

For the next several days we followed the shoreline in a southwesterly direction, waking up each morning in a warmer and greener country.

Finally we turned inland, heading up a small river. After paddling as far as we could we left the canoes behind and continued on foot. After a few more days spent crossing a flat and treeless land we came to the mouth of a creek, where Ahareehon instructed us to make camp.

"Be careful not to speak or make any noise," he said. "We're close to the enemy now."

After a light supper, we spread out to look for signs of them. Though we found nothing we went to sleep with a feeling of satisfaction, sure at last we had arrived in the land of the Erie.

The next morning we followed the stream which ended in a small lake. Searching along the shore we encountered fresh footprints leading away from it, which we followed to the banks of another small river where we almost ran into an old woman bent over under a bundle of sticks. As she hadn't seen us, we let her pass by.

"She may be on the way back to her village," Ahareehon said. "At the very least, there must be a cabin for shelter nearby. Wait here while I go ahead and see what I can find out." He returned shortly, saying he had seen five men and four women fishing on the side of the river.

Before beginning the attack, we sat in a circle to plan the best means to surprise our intended prey.

At the conclusion of our meeting, Ahareehon said, "We'll sneak up and pounce on them like hungry wolves. Then devour them quickly and quietly, giving them no time to warn their comrades. As there are nine of them and eleven of us, Ovinha and the Oneida boy will stay here to watch and learn."

The Erie stood idly by the side of the river watching over their nets while Ahareehon and the others just a few feet away crouched in the grass behind them. I watched as our men silently pointed out their victims. Then as soon as Ahareehon gave the signal they sprang from their hiding places, and cut the throats of the five men and four women before they even saw their executioners. As planned, they expired without a sound.

The loot we got from this carnage wasn't much. Only a few deerskins and belts made of goat's hair, which the Mohawk valued for its rarity and skillful workmanship. After cutting away their scalps, we threw their bodies into the river.

Emboldened by such an easy victory, we went to look for more scalps and plunder. Following a narrow path beside the river, we came to another small lake where we turned into the woods along a wide trail, worn from frequent use. At dusk we reached the outskirts of an unprotected village.

After searching in the darkness for a place to spend the night, we made shelters in a clearing about half a mile from the village. Then, after enjoying a meal of the Erie fishermen's catch we were thirsty and sent a volunteer to look for water.

Before long he returned with some and the news, all was quiet in the hamlet. Sure the Erie were unaware of our presence, we retired for the night.

The next morning we hid in the trees beside some cultivated fields waiting for someone to come. Early in the afternoon we noticed movement in the distance; then after sneaking through the woods for a closer look, we observed about twenty men and women at work.

From our hiding place we watched them tend their crops. Corn stalks, already a few inches high, sprouted on mounds of dirt alongside spreading vines of beans and squash.

While the Erie passed the afternoon peacefully cultivating their fields, we waited patiently to kill them.

At last, as the setting sun turned tree tops gold and soil the color of dried blood, the Erie put down their implements and went into the woods to gather fuel for the evening.

Three women approached the spot where we lay hidden. Then one of them, bending down to pick up a stick, saw us and screamed.

We followed them as they ran to their village, where men with bows and arrows came out to meet us.

The battle was short and fierce. Although the Erie defended themselves bravely, their arrows were no match for our bullets. When they saw their comrades falling all around them, the survivors fled in terror.

Their stone-tipped arrows wounded five of our men. Though most of our injuries were slight, the Oneida boy was horribly wounded with two arrows in his back and his skull crushed in. As he lay bleeding and moaning – to end his misery – Ahareehon shot him in the head.

"If he had only held his ground like the rest of us he might still be alive," Ahareehon said afterwards. Everyone agreed he deserved his fate.

In the brief skirmish we killed two of them and took five captives. This time our plunder was considerable. Among the things we acquired were two sacks of corn, several rolls of deerhide, some clay pipes, turquoise, tobacco, and several belts, garters, and necklaces made of the goat's hair we admired.

Many of the Erie wore headdresses made from strips of snakeskin decorated with bears' paws, and some of them wore their hair long. As we gathered up the booty and tied the prisoners, we affirmed to one another the enemy put up a good fight and were all real men.

Before the Erie were able to return with reinforcements, we retreated from the scene of battle. Stopping neither to eat nor drink nor rest, three days later we reached the place where we left the canoes. Then after a little supper we went to sleep, exhausted.

In the middle of the night we got up and continued. The campaign against the Erie was over, and now all we wanted was to get as far away from their country as we could.

It took nearly three weeks to reach the end of Lake Ontario and the river that would take us near our homes in the Mohawk Valley. Our journey ended at the bottom of a high waterfall, where we landed the canoes and sent for our women. As Anihé wasn't far away they arrived shortly. After such a lengthy separation we were excited to see them again, and when I saw Conharrasan and Gahano with them I ran to take them in my arms.

Chapter Nine
Victory Celebrations

"With a fearsome war cry the Erie captain ran towards him. But Ovinha stood his ground and waited until the captain – with hatchet raised, and ready to strike – was only two strides away. Then, taking careful aim, Ovinha fired and the captain fell dead at his feet."

When Ahareehon finished recounting my small victory for the benefit of our women my fellow warriors shouted, "Hail Devil Ovinha." Sitting by my side, Conharrasan and Gahano beamed with pride.

They had brought me presents, including a new white shirt from Fort Orange. I in turn gave them the Erie captain's scalp and six deerskins, "to make new dresses with," I said.

Besides these things my share of the plunder from our foray into Erie country was twenty beaver pelts, three bear skins and some moose grease, as well as various belts and necklaces we took from the Erie. I also kept a female prisoner to be my mother's servant.

When darkness fell we made a roaring fire on the beach by the waterfall. Then, happy to be safe and back with our girlfriends and wives, we sang and danced around it far into the night. At last, very late, we retired to our beds.

I followed Conharrasan and Gahano down the beach to a secluded spot where they had fashioned a mattress out of pine boughs covered with deerskins.

After we had lain down, with me in the middle, they took my moccasins off and covered us with a woolen blanket even though it was a warm summer night.

"I'm too hot," I said before long.

"We can take care of that," Conharrasan said. Then she and Gahano removed the rest of my scant clothing, before undressing themselves.

"Isn't this better," Conharrasan said, pressing the length of her body against my bare flesh.

"Did you miss us," Gahano said, at the same time lightly touching my skin all over.

"Every night," I said, finding it harder and harder to think as my desire grew. "Before I went to sleep . . . when I missed you most . . . course, during . . . day . . . busy . . . fighting . . . Erie . . . think . . . lovers."

"Oh, Conharrasan, isn't Ovinha brave," Gahano said.

"Brave and generous, too. I think we should reward him for his courage and good nature."

"I think so too."

Then they began to kiss me everywhere. Finally,

when I could no longer endure such sweet torture I took them in my arms, first one and then the other, and we made love until dawn.

It was mid-day when I woke up. Looking around, I saw a pot hanging over the fire and Conharrasan and Gahano in the river, splashing one another and squealing like children.

Sitting up on our bed of pine needles, I admired their beauty. Water on bare skin reflecting the sun's rays like wet copper. Conharrasan soft and round, Gahano taller and firmer than when I left. Shiny black hair falling to their waists.

How fortunate I am, I thought. Two beautiful women who love me, parents who spoil me, and a brother and companions, all loyal and true. What a life I lead.

I could hardly imagine a happier existence. A Mohawk warrior now, I enjoyed all the privileges and pleasures accorded my rank. Bold and brave on the warpath we went hungry, without water and without sleep. While at home we ate whenever we wanted to, drank as we pleased, and made love to our women as often as we desired.

"Come and join us," my two lovers called. Though a little reluctant to leave our comfortable bed I got up and waded into the river, where they greeted me with warm kisses and a refreshing bath in the clear stream.

Later I sat in the sun while they combed and greased my hair. Then, after pronouncing themselves satisfied with my appearance, they brought me some boiled meat.

We stayed four days by the waterfall, enjoying ourselves each day as on the first. All day long we danced and sang, while gorging ourselves on wild game and reliving our victories. Then, before we slept, we made love to our women. Finally, when we were ready to leave, they gathered up our things and painted us with war paint for the return to Anihé.

Like a Roman legion we entered in triumph. Word of our arrival having spread quickly, many of the inhabitants were at the gates to greet us. The first time I entered this village I had been consumed with fear but now, with my arms around Conharrasan's and Gahano's waists, and a crowd gathered not to torture me but to welcome me back, I experienced the pleasure of returning home after a long absence.

As we marched past the throng of spectators they hailed us by name with praises for our courage. But the loudest exclamations were reserved for me. From all sides I heard them chant, "Be cheerful Devil Ovinha," the whole village by then having heard of my deeds.

Gannendaris was waiting for us near the gates,

where a mob had gathered to torment the prisoners. When she saw us, she began to leap up and down and sing with joy.

"Look what I've brought you, mother," I said, after we had embraced, showing her first three skins full of grease. "For the household," I said. Then, "And here, this healthy young woman to help you with your work."

Taking hold of the Erie woman's trembling hand Gannendaris said, "Have no fear, my child, no one shall touch a hair on your head."

But Aweegatay's prisoner wasn't so fortunate. After giving Gannendaris his two scalps he turned his prisoner over to the mob who took him along with the other prisoners to scaffolds in an open space where fires of hell burned. There, as I later heard, they beat him and plucked out his nails and poked him with hot sticks, his screams and death song mingling with those of the other victims. And finally, before he could expire from his wounds, they burned him alive at the stake.

After our return the festivities continued. Daily we had banquets to celebrate our conquests and safe return. From dawn until midnight we ate, sang, gambled and played games, or danced around the scalps of our enemies.

Many young men and women came especially to learn about my modest exploits. They brought me treats and sat with rapt attention while I repeated the stories of our victorious campaign.

Finally, growing tired of these entertainments, we decided to go to Fort Orange to trade our beaver pelts and to amuse ourselves at the expense of the Dutch.

Chapter Ten
Dutch Hospitality

Since my father had not yet returned from the war against the Algonquin and the French, I left for Fort Orange without his permission.

On the second day after our departure, our band of ten young men marched into a small outlying settlement with only a few houses. We entered each without being invited, and the Dutch – unwilling or unable to stand in our way – greeted us warmly, treating us as though we were expected guests.

With barely a frown they watched as we peered into simmering pots, lifting lids up and down, and picking out pieces of meat with our hands. Then banging cupboard doors open and shut in search of whatever we could find to satisfy our appetites or quench our thirst.

We helped ourselves to their wine and soon my companions were drunk and quarreling among themselves. When they began waving their knives around, the Dutch looked uneasy.

No one threatened me, however, and I paid no attention to their squabbles. In fact, though I drank as much as they did I remained sober. The difference was I drank my wine slowly, always nibbling on something, while they guzzled theirs without eating.

On the fourth day of our visit – having

frightened more settlers along the way – we entered Fort Orange, the principal settlement of New Holland. It was where the Mohawk came to exchange beaver skins – mostly pillaged from their enemies – for guns and household items. Since both sides profited from the trade, upon our arrival with two hundred prime pelts the inhabitants received us warmly.

They invited us into their homes where they plied us with dried prunes and raisins and filled our pipes with tobacco. "Trade your beaver pelts with us," the host, or hostess, of each house said. But resisting the temptation to turn a quick profit, we went from house to house offering nothing in exchange for their treats other than a "ho, ho," to express our gratitude for their generosity.

With Aweegatay I entered another house, where the hostess was a middle-aged Scottish widow. While some of her guests – both men and women – plied my brother and me with treats, a French soldier standing to the side studied me closely. Finally, after a few minutes of looking me up and down, he approached our little circle.

"For all your paint and grease," he said in the Iroquois tongue, "you don't look Mohawk to me. In reality you are a Frenchman, are you not?"

"No, I am not," I said abruptly in Iroquois.

"Merde," he said. Then, continuing in French, "How did you ever fall into the hands of such a people?"

Surprised to hear my native tongue, which I had not heard for more than a year, I could no longer hide my true identity.

"Yes," I said in French, "I am indeed, as you guessed, myself French."

"Mon Dieu, it's true then, you are French like me," the soldier said. Then, overcome with emotion, he threw his arms around me. I grasped him in return, surprised by the warmth of feeling embracing a fellow countryman gave me.

"Listen up, everyone," he said, when he had recovered a little of his composure. "This wild boy is not what he seems, for in truth he is a Frenchman just like me." Upon which everyone in the room turned to one another with astonished looks.

"But look at you," he said, turning to me again. "You are as fearsome looking as any wild man who ever stepped out of the forest. Tell me, how did you ever come to be in such a state?"

My countryman's reproach made me blush with shame. Then, having overcome his initial shock, the soldier proposed a toast, "To the Frenchman in disguise," he said to the assembled guests.

Whereupon everyone in the room gathered round me, Dutch and French alike, for as it turned out the soldier who recognized me was not the only one of my countrymen present. Holding out their bottles they invited me to drink, all of them saying they were willing to help me in whatever way they could.

News I was French spread through the hamlet quickly. Kind Flemish ladies vied with one another to be the first to invite me into their homes where they gave me the best of what they had. I ate their bread and meat, while their husbands filled my glass with beer and my pipe with tobacco. As I made the rounds, my Mohawk companions followed me through the streets in a pack, observing my behavior as if I was some sort of strange specimen.

I was taken to see the Governor. Seated behind a large desk he had a somewhat comic appearance, with a burgundy velvet waistcoat and a white silk shirt with a starched collar folded like an accordion and a red face perched on top. His hair, cropped short, was red like his neat moustache and beard trimmed to a point. The Governor, who spoke French as well as a Frenchman, rose and greeted me warmly.

"Well young man," he said after we were seated, "please tell us all about your adventures. For anything that concerns the Iroquois and the beaver trade also concerns us."

Sitting across from the Governor with nothing to hide my nakedness but my breechcloth and painted face, I told him the kind of life I led as a young

Mohawk warrior. He seemed fascinated, interrupting me more than once with polite inquiries regarding certain particulars of my narrative.

My journey across the upper country to the land of the Erie interested him a great deal, and he asked many questions about it. Was the climate there temperate, did I think it suitable for farming, were there beaver there, by what route did we go, and the like. At the end of our conversation, which lasted more than an hour, the Governor offered to buy my freedom.

"We could use a man like you here," he said. "Your knowledge of the country as well as their language and customs would be valuable to our fur trade. As you've seen, some of your countrymen already bring their furs to us, claiming they have been treated unfairly in New France. Ask your fellows what ransom they want for you. No matter the price, we will gladly pay it. Or, if they refuse, we can free you from their clutches by the force of arms."

"Sir," I said, after considering it, "though your offer is extremely generous, I am not yet ready to leave these people. They have been good to me, and I love my adopted parents as I once loved my natural ones. Perhaps it is God's will I stay with them for it seems to be my destiny to discover new nations."

"As you wish, although I am sorry to see you go. Nevertheless, I am confident you will be successful in whatever you choose to do. And, remember, if you should ever change your mind, our offer will still be good."

Afterwards, my companions and I prepared to return to Anihé. We had done well in Fort Orange and looked forward to spending the winter with our women. We hoped, too, to find our fathers returned from the war against the Algonquin and the French.

As we left, the Frenchman who discovered my true identity tried to persuade me to change my mind. "You'll break their hearts," he said, pointing to the Flemish ladies standing in doorways who had taken me into their homes. "Look, how they cry to see you leave in such a company of wolves." But, though his entreaties brought tears to my eyes, I remained firm in my decision.

Two days later, with no stops on the way, we were reunited with our loved ones. I turned over all my earnings to Conharrasan and Gahano leaving it to them to distribute them among the household as they saw fit. As always they gave me more than my share for they were too generous to me, as I was to them.

Chapter Eleven
Escape From Anihé

Not long after our return I began to be sorry I hadn't accepted the Governor's offer. The short time I spent with the Dutch had brought back fond memories of the decency and kindness of my own French compatriots. It reminded me too of the gentleness of my sister, while giving me hope I might one day see her again.

Thinking about the goodness of the French and the Dutch, I reflected on what might become of me if I continued to live among a people who could be so pitiless. With these thoughts pulling me away, only the love I felt for my Mohawk family kept me from immediately leaving again.

But as days went by, still without word from my father's army, I began to fear what the Iroquois would do to me if they learned the Algonquin and the French defeated them. Having many times witnessed their cruelty, I resolved not to wait to find out.

For these reasons and the nearness of Fort Orange, I made up my mind to escape as soon as possible. All the while I kept my thoughts from my family, though I felt badly for having to deceive them this way.

Then early one morning, less than two weeks after returning from Fort Orange, I started back. All day and night I ran through the woods without stopping until finally, weak and faint with hunger, I had to stop and rest. Then, as soon as the sun was up, I resumed my way. Again I ran all day, finding the strength to go on from my fear and from my desire for a new beginning.

Finally, late in the afternoon of the second day, I came to the edge of a clearing. Staying out of sight behind some trees I observed a man hard at work cutting wood. Moving closer, I called to him.

"I have some beaver to trade," I said in Iroquois as he came towards me.

"Well," he said, having taken me for a Mohawk, "bring them up to the house, where we may conduct our business in comfort."

"First you must swear none of my brothers are there."

"There's nothing to worry about," he said. "Except for my wife, I am alone. Bring your pelts inside where I promise you will be well looked after."

"As I've hidden them in the woods, I'll bring them in the morning. But for now I would be grateful for a little food and drink."

"Of course, come with me and we'll provide you with some nourishment."

I followed the man into their modest dwelling where his wife gave me the best of what they had, which wasn't much as they were quite poor.

When I had finished eating, I asked for pen and ink and a piece of paper. As this request seemed to astonish my hosts, I explained that though a Mohawk I had lived for a while among the French and had something of importance to communicate to the Governor.

Though they had never before seen a Mohawk who could either read or write, they furnished me with the necessary materials and watched in admiration while I composed an urgent appeal to the Governor.

When I finished, it gave me great satisfaction to see my French name again, having signed the letter, "Your humble servant, Pierre Esprit Radisson."

After making the Dutchman promise to go straight to the Governor's house without stopping along the way or telling anyone where I was, I gave him the letter. "I shouldn't be long," he said on his way out. "The fort is barely two miles from here."

After her husband was gone his attractive young wife – believing the story I told them – said, "Tell me, if you don't mind, when you were with the French how did you pass the time?" And, when I didn't reply, "Perhaps the French ladies invited you to sleep with them?"

But I was too afraid for my life to respond in the way she desired, and when a company of Mohawk passed by singing loudly I was no longer able to contain my fear. "Please kind lady," I said, "hide me somewhere where my countrymen can't find me. If they do they will kill me for running away from them to be with the Dutch and the French."

When the good woman realized how terrified I was she hid me in a corner behind two sacks of grain where I remained trembling with fright until her husband returned.

The French soldier who had guessed my true nationality and two others were with him. After putting on the clothes they brought to disguise me in case we met any Iroquois along the way, I bade farewell to my hosts. Then, after apologizing for having nothing to offer except my gratitude, I went with my escorts to see the Governor.

"Well Pierre, I'm pleased you've changed your mind," he said, after hearing my plans, "although I'm sorry you won't be staying with us for long. Until, according to your wishes, we are able to arrange for your return to France, a retired merchant from Brussels, a Catholic who's fluent in French, has offered to put you up. As he is engaged in the fur trade, I'm sure your knowledge of the Iroquois will be sufficient recompense for your room and board. Now, as I see it is late and you must be extremely tired from your ordeals, I'll bid you goodnight. Tomorrow one of my men will bring you some new clothes."

The next morning, after putting on the suit the Governor sent and cleaning away all the paint and grease from my former life, I looked at myself in a mirror. An apparition stared back. Gone the deerhide leggings and breechcloth; my moccasins and loose fitting white linen shirt. What I saw standing in my place was a typical Dutchman wearing a snug fitting waistcoat, breeches to his knees, long stockings held in place with garters, and a pair of leather shoes. This fellow's face was scrubbed clean, unlike the smudged one of his former self.

I stood in front of the mirror awhile, unable to decide which of me I liked best. The me before or the me now, although I was certain which one my dear Mohawk sisters would have preferred if they had been there.

As I made my way to the house where the French soldier was boarding with the kind Scottish widow my new clothes felt tight and the hard leather shoes uncomfortable.

"I can't believe how much your appearance has changed. Yesterday anyone but me would have sworn you were a Mohawk. Now you wouldn't be out of place in the salons of France," my new friend said after letting me in.

"You'll stay for dinner, won't you? I'm sure you'll enjoy the food we have simmering over the hearth, and find the guest who has just arrived of interest."

The other guest was an old Jesuit priest by the name of Father Joseph Poncet, released that day from the Mohawk who captured him near Québec at the end of August. After we had enjoyed the Scottish lady's delicious venison stew and moved to her comfortable parlor, where she offered us some of her imported apples, Father Poncet said, "Pierre, please tell us how you fell into the hands of these heathens," which was what he called the Iroquois.

Then for the first time since the Mohawk took me more than a year ago I was able to tell the story of my captivity to a sympathetic audience. "On a fine day in May of last year I left Trois Rivières to hunt along the river with two of my companions," I began.

"By the end of the morning when my friends said they wanted to go back and after we had quarreled about it awhile we parted company. Then later in the afternoon, when I was also on my way back to the fort, I discovered their bodies beside a pond . . . "

The others leaned forward as I continued recounting the details of my captivity – describing my companions' horrible wounds; then how the Mohawk had pounced on me, and our subsequent journey to their country. I recalled our arrival in Anihé, where an angry mob waited to beat me; then the unexpected appearance of Aweegatay's mother, who became my protector and my adopted mother.

My audience listened without interruption while I related the rest of the time I spent with the Mohawk, right up to the present. Except for the intimate details of my relationship with Conharrasan and Gahano, I left nothing out.

From their expressions I could tell they were shocked. In particular, my experiences on the warpath against the Erie made the Scottish lady shudder, and when I finished my account she hurried to say, "Young man, I find it difficult to comprehend how a good Christian like yourself could have slaughtered innocent women and children. Did your conscience not trouble you?"

"No madam," I said. "In fact, no longer thinking of myself as French, I was able to kill without remorse because this was what was expected of the Mohawk warrior I had become. Perhaps, owing to my youth, I adapted too easily to Mohawk ways – including the killing and torturing of their enemies."

"Remember, dear lady," the French soldier said, "that it wasn't that long ago that good Catholics gathered to witness the persecution and burning of their own neighbours, accused not of murder but merely suspected of being heretics or witches. I'm afraid we are not as far from being like the Iroquois as we like to think."

"Still, it would be hard to surpass them in the realm of torture. The Iroquois are the masters of terror," Father Poncet said. "I should know, as I speak from experience. If you will permit me I would like to share with you my own acquaintance with their cruelty."

"Of course, please tell us about it," the French soldier said, to which we all added our encouragement.

"On our way to a different village than the one Pierre was taken to, the heathen who captured me took away a copper box in which I carried all the necessities of our trade – a Catechism, some holy water, a Crucifix, and the like – as well as a wooden cross and a medallion of our Holy Saint Mary from around my neck, which he put around his own."

By his face we could see the pain his losses brought. Continuing, he said, "Then one day as the heathens were running through the woods with the prisoners in tow, the box opened up and all the relics were lost."

"You poor man," the Scottish lady couldn't help from saying. "You must have been terribly frightened."

"It was, madam, a difficult time, indeed. But, to return to our voyage, when we came to some rapids they ordered me out of our canoe and compelled me to cross on foot. The water went up to my waist and this together with the lack of food made me have severe stomach aches and bowel disorders and great pains all over. Nevertheless, I continued all my usual devotions, consoling myself quietly with thoughts of the sufferings of our Savior."

Again the Scottish woman, much moved by the Father's story, expressed her sympathy. "How dreadful," she said.

Father Poncet nodded in polite agreement and continued his narrative, providing us with further details of the difficulties of the journey to their destination, the Mohawk village where a horde of tormentors at the entrance made him and the other prisoners run through a gauntlet, beating them as they passed by. Then made them climb a scaffold in the middle of a square to insult and torment them some more.

Finally Father Poncet came to the climax of his account. "In the evening they took me inside a lodge where some elders were assembled. A woman among them offered a bracelet of wampum to have my finger cut off. And so the brute who had captured me took my right hand and considered it. Then, just as I was thinking that the fingers of that hand were a little more useful to me than those of the left, he let go of it and called over his son, a child of four or five, and handed him a knife and told him to cut off the little finger of my left hand. As the child sawed away at it I sang with all my heart for the glory of Our Lord Jesus Christ, and willingly sacrificed my blood and suffering for peace."

At this point he stopped to show us where the

little finger of his left hand had been cut off, just above the first knuckle.

"How terrible," the Scottish lady said, "how you must have suffered."

"It was all in the service of God," Father Poncet said. "For by then I had formed the opinion that I should afterwards work for peace. To this end I believe it was necessary I carry some scars, and is why God willed they cut off one of my fingers . . . Madam, might I help myself to another apple? It's been fifteen years since I've tasted one."

As the good Father's accounts were lengthy, the afternoon passed by quickly, and as evening was fast approaching, I told them I had to be going, having no desire to encounter any of my former countrymen in the dark.

"Perhaps in the morning you would be disposed to let me hear your confession," Father Poncet said as I was leaving. "Tomorrow is Sunday, and as I have no parish to preach to it would be my pleasure to help set your mind at peace."

Considering his offer, I thought it might do me some good. For to tell the truth – having returned to a world that saw things differently than the Iroquois – I had begun to be troubled by some of the crimes I committed while I lived with them.

"Thank you Father. I'd like that. I'll come to see you tomorrow," I said.

The following day, with the merchant's help, I was so busy making arrangements for my departure the day slipped by without my going to see Father Poncet. I was somewhat surprised, then, when towards evening he appeared at our door in the company of the merchant's assistant, an old Huron.

"It is our Savior who has brought me to stay with you," he said as he came in, "for the day I was set free was also the birthday of the Lord's mother, our Lady of Grace."

Only later did I learn the truth of how he came to join me in the merchant's house, that he had gone to the Governor and asked him to recommend him to the merchant, telling him he was without food and had no place to sleep except on the floor.

"Before we begin, a little supper might help to put us in the proper frame of mind," he said in a loud voice. Providentially, the merchant soon summoned us to dinner. After we had eaten, the good Father said he would take a short nap first as it was better to pray on an empty stomach.

The next day, still not having heard my confession, Father Poncet thought he might be able to perform his office better with the proper equipment. The Scottish lady, who was disappointed to have lost her charming guest to the wealthy merchant, found him a black coat to use in place of the usual Jesuit cassock, while the merchant took time from his business to look for a St. Jerome

Latin edition of the Bible, a book hard to find in Protestant New Holland.

As these activities took up much of the day Father Poncet thought we should make a fresh start in the morning. Finally, on the third day of his stay with us, I was able to tell him some of the things troubling my conscience.

What troubled me most was my part in murdering the Erie, innocent people who had never done us harm. Though I'm sure Father Poncet would not have approved, I didn't believe the intimacy I shared with my Mohawk sisters a sin, and kept it to myself.

Perhaps, because of his own sufferings, Father Poncet was understanding and forgiving. "The Iroquois are heathens," he said, "who have not yet benefited from Christian instruction. Your sin in killing the Erie captain, as serious as it is, must be considered in this light. If it had been a Christian you had killed rather than a heathen then, my son, your sins would be unforgivable and no earthly intervention could ever save you from eternal damnation in hell. But as you are an otherwise worthy Catholic who has gone astray, I see no reason why God shouldn't forgive you. Do you repent your sins, then?"

"Yes Father, with all my heart."

"Then, as your penance you must help us to convert the heathens. An Iroquois delegation has gone to Québec to talk peace, which was the reason the Mohawk set me free. Meanwhile the Company of Jesus is making preparations to send priests to their villages to make Christians of them. Laymen such as yourself will be needed for this great venture, and it is therefore God's wish that you put your knowledge of their language and country at His service.

"When you reach New France go to Québec, where Father Ragueneau will be waiting to hear from you."

"As soon as I am able to I will do as you and God command."

"Well," he said, "I feel much better now, don't you? It's good to relieve one's mind of these burdens. By the way, do you have a patron saint?"

"No, Father, I don't."

"Then I can recommend no better benefactress than our Virgin Mother. Here, take this medallion and wear it around your neck," he said, and gave me a thin brass pendant engraved with an image of the Blessed Saint Mary.

The next day, after thanking everyone for their kindness, I took a barge down the Hudson River to New Amsterdam – now New York – which had decent amenities for a new country, including taverns where I was able to drink more good Dutch beer.

At the end of October I boarded a ship for Holland. Then after a cold and stormy crossing I found another boat that took me to the fishing port of La Rochelle, France, from where as soon as possible I left on a ship bound for Percé in the Gulf of St. Lawrence.

Arriving at the beginning of May, I searched the small fishing village for the means to be near to my relatives and countrymen again. At last I found passage with a flotilla of Algonquin canoes which with the aid of a favorable northeast wind brought us to Québec in a few days time.

From there I made my way to Trois Rivières, arriving two years after being carried away. There, with many joyful tears on both sides, I was reunited with my sister and her children, whom I never thought to see again.

In time I saw Father Poncet again and he told me how, three days after my departure, my Mohawk friends and relatives had come to look for me in Fort Orange.

"The two girls who were your adopted sisters wandered the streets crying out your name," he said. "Everyone was astounded to see them make such a display of grief, and we couldn't help wondering what made them love you so much."

I knew the reason, though, and with longing in my heart I too lamented having lost the love we shared.

PART TWO

FRENCH ADVENTURES

Chapter Twelve
My New Brother-In-Law

Trois Rivières, New France – 1654

New France was at peace. The Confederation representing the five Iroquois nations – the Mohawk, the Oneida, the Onondaga, the Cayuga, and the Seneca – had sought a truce, and the inhabitants welcomed it.

The other piece of good news I had was my sister had remarried. I was happy for her, as she had suffered so much. Four years earlier the Iroquois murdered her first husband, Jean Véron. Then, widowed at twenty and alone with two small children, she wrote to me in France asking for my help, which is how I came to live with her in Trois Rivières.

Now sitting in front of the fireplace the evening of my first day back, our troubles seemed behind us. In a bedroom of Marguérite's new and larger cabin, her three boys slept peacefully.

With the children quiet, we had time to fill in the gaps of snatches of conversation we had throughout a busy day.

"After the Iroquois took you with them I was heartsick," Marguérite said. "Though I never lost hope you would come back. Now here you are, and I can't believe how much you've changed. You left a boy and came back a man. Taller and stronger and even better looking than before. But most of all you seem more mature, more thoughtful. You were so impetuous before."

"Well, I am two years older," I said.

"Still, I bet those Mohawk girls had something to do with it," Marguérite said, a twinkle in her light blue eyes.

"They were good company," I said. "But they weren't the only reason I grew up quickly. In the situation I found myself in I had to understand how others felt and thought. In this respect, my Mohawk mother was a good teacher as was my Mohawk father. And from my brother and his friends I learned how to track and catch animals, which taught me patience."

"Did your Mohawk parents treat you well?" Marguérite asked.

"They were very good to me. It may surprise you that the Iroquois, who are renowned for their cruelty, are generous to one another."

"Speaking of their cruelty which, sadly, I know better than their kindness, earlier today you told me you went with a band of young men to fight one of their enemies. How did that happen?"

"After I was formally accepted into my family and the Mohawk nation, my father let me go with my adopted brother to fight the Erie. In their eyes, when I became a warrior I also became a man."

"You know how I feel about the Iroquois," Marguérite said, "but your life with them sounds so exciting I wonder why you didn't stay. By the time you decided to escape you were a hero, with two Mohawk girls who adored you."

"I told you how worried I was when my Mohawk father failed to return from the war against the French. But it was also during my first visit to Fort Orange, when that Frenchman I told you about recognized me, that I had a chance to compare the simple life I was leading as a Mohawk with the civilized one of the French and the Dutch. This and my father's continued absence made me determined to escape. It wasn't easy leaving behind a family I loved, but I also thought of you and my nephews and how much I cared for you, and you for me."

"I'm happy you remembered us. We never forgot you or gave up hope. I'm sure you'll find a use here for all you've learned while you were away. My husband, for one, will be very interested in your experiences, as he also has a great deal of knowledge of the native people. When he gets back from Montréal, where he has gone to see Charles Le Moyne, his business partner in a voyage he is about to make in the west, I am sure you and he will have much to talk about."

"You may be right. In Fort Orange after my escape I discovered I had something of value to offer. Both the Governor there and Father Poncet wanted to make use of the knowledge I had of the

Iroquois, and I am sure your husband will want to as well. Now, Marguérite, tell me more about him. What's he like?"

"Well," Marguérite said, "to start with, his full name is Médard Chouart, Sieur Des Groseilliers . . . "

"He has a title?"

"A minor one, really. However, it's enough to base his hopes on of someday being a seigneur."

"He sounds ambitious."

"He is, and determined too. When his mind is made up he won't listen to anyone. Then, let me tell you, it takes a brave soul to stand up to him."

"Well, I am sure he's met his match in you."

Marguérite laughed, and said, "That may be true, although we have had our differences. In particular, over his treatment of our two oldest boys by his first marriage."

"He's older than you, then?"

"Yes, he is thirty-six, twelve years older than myself, which may be why he thought he knew better than me how to raise children. Although he has a good heart he can be too strict. But I hope I am not painting too disagreeable a picture of my husband, for I would not have married him if his shortcomings were not far outweighed by his good qualities. I love him very much, as I am sure you will too."

Soon after Médard's return from Montréal, my nephew Jean Baptiste was christened. In the small log chapel inside the walls of Trois Rivières his parents beamed with pride throughout the baptism ceremony of the first child born to their sometimes stormy union.

After the service, I joined my brother-in-law outside our cabin where we went for some air, having just celebrated the baptism at a splendid table. With a jug of brandy between us we discussed the state of affairs in New France and plans for the future.

"Well, Pierre, now that we are part of the same family, let us call one another brother."

"I would like that," I said.

"It was good of you to return from your adventures with the Mohawk to be with us for this joyful occasion. Though if you had only delayed your escape another year you might have come back with them and saved yourself a lot of trouble."

"You refer to the peace with the Iroquois; what do you know about it?"

"As you might have imagined from your vantage point in the heart of Mohawk country, last year was a bad one for New France. When I returned last summer with what furs I could find I had never seen morale so low. The Algonquin nations from the west no longer dared bring their furs to us, and the warehouses of New France were empty. The colony was facing ruin and many inhabitants talked openly of abandoning it."

Médard paused to take a swig of brandy. We were seated on the ground, our backs against the wall of Marguérite's log cabin. After using the back of his sleeve to wipe away some drops of brandy from his dark beard, he resumed his account. "As it turned out," he said, "the war had been damaging to both sides. The Iroquois suffered many losses and . . ."

"I can confirm the truth of that. My Mohawk father who was a great warrior-chief led an army in the spring against the Algonquin and the French. Last September, when they still had not returned, my fear of what they might do to me if it turned out he had been killed was one of the reasons I ran away."

"While at the same time I was defending Trois Rivières against the onslaught of your father's army," Médard said. "I killed many of the Iroquois myself – both Mohawk and Onondaga. As a result of our vigorous defense, at the end of last summer the Onondaga sent emissaries to Québec to propose a truce."

"Early last year I passed through where the Onondaga live and I can tell you they inhabit a fine country at the center of the Iroquois Confederacy," I said.

"Yes, and now they want us to go and settle among them," Médard said.

"It sounds suspicious. What do you think their purpose can be? After all, the Mohawk have sworn to drive us all back to France."

"Exactly, and that is what concerns Governor Lauzon, too. But the Jesuits are convinced we should take advantage of the Onondaga offer. They have even gone so far as to send Father Simon Le Moyne to Onondaga to determine if a mission can be established there."

"I got to know him in Québec after I arrived from France," I said. "I learned much about the Iroquois from him, never imagining I would soon be living with them. He is familiar with native customs and traditions, and his knowledge of the Huron and Iroquois languages is extensive. If anyone can persuade the Iroquois to become Christians it is he."

"Which is what the Jesuits are hoping for. Ever since Sainte-Marie among the Huron was destroyed, our poor Fathers have been without souls to save. And now that they see a chance to make new converts they are anxious to found a new mission even if it means being martyred along the way."

Taking another swallow from the brandy I

hardly touched – much preferring beer – Médard chuckled to himself, for it seemed his long association with the Jesuits had made him skeptical of their motives. As for myself, my faith in the good Fathers was then unquestioning.

"Well, having seen how cruel the Iroquois can be, I certainly have no desire to be martyred. Though I do agree it might be to our benefit to be allies with them rather than remain enemies."

"An alliance with the upper Iroquois would certainly be to our advantage," Médard said. "As it would give us access to other nations and to more beaver pelts. But until we are sure this peace is genuine we will have to go west ourselves to where the Algonquin-speaking nations – the Ottawa, the Ojibway, and others – who used to live on the eastern side of Lake Huron, have settled since the Iroquois drove them from their homes.

"Although last year a small party of Ottawa did arrive from the west. They said they would come back again this summer with pelts they have been accumulating since the beginning of the war with the Iroquois. They told me, since fleeing the Iroquois, they have been gathering in large numbers in a fine country about four hundred miles west of the west side of Lake Huron. They want guns and ammunition to defend themselves against the Iroquois with whom they are still at war as the current peace is only with us and the Huron, who are too weak now to matter. If they come I intend to return with them."

"I would love to go with you," I said. "Even though I have promised to help the Jesuits establish their new mission among the upper Iroquois."

"One day you shall have your wish," Médard said, "but for the present you must stay here. The Governor has granted Charles Le Moyne and me the exclusive right to trade with the Ottawa and other Algonquin-speaking nations in the west. Monsieur Le Moyne will send a representative to accompany me as he must stay behind for the defense of Montréal.

"We also have to consider Marguérite's wishes. I don't think she would be too pleased if you went with me now, so soon after escaping the Iroquois. Even if I could take you I would not want to risk the household peace. No, little brother, stay here where you can be more useful. Help Marguérite with the children. Keep the table full of meat. Meanwhile, I am sure the Holy Fathers will want to make good use of your knowledge of the Iroquois. Then, next summer, when I return with a king's ransom's worth of beaver pelts, we will build a manor together that will be the envy of all of New France."

The Ottawa came at the beginning of August. And as promised their canoes were loaded with furs for which they were paid with the guns and ammunition they came for. When they re-embarked on the St. Lawrence River to begin the long journey home Médard went with them. In Montréal they would meet Charles Le Moyne's man.

I stood at the water's edge with Marguérite and the rest of the inhabitants of our small settlement who had come to see them off. Upon reaching the middle of the river they stopped and let out a succession of whoops, while simultaneously raising their paddles in a final salute. From shore we answered with our guns.

Then, they were off. As we watched Médard and the Ottawa disappear over the horizon Marguérite fought back her tears while I vowed to myself, *the next time he goes I'll go with him.*

Chapter Thirteen
Father Ragueneau

Soon after Médard and the Ottawa left, I went to see Father Paul Ragueneau in Québec.

He lived in the Jesuit residence in upper town just below Fort St. Louis, the administrative and military headquarters of New France. To reach the heights of Cape Diamond, where Fort St. Louis overlooked the St. Lawrence River, I climbed up a steep and winding road from the docks and warehouses below.

Father Ragueneau wore the priest's customary black habit with a plain wooden crucifix hanging from his neck. His hair, cut short, was sparse on top and graying at the temples. His face also thin but with a gentle appearance.

We sat in his white plastered room, furnished with only a bed, a writing table, and two wooden stools.

"I have been expecting you," he said after I introduced myself. "You come highly recommended. Father Poncet thinks you will be of great help with our plans to convert the Iroquois."

"I lived as one of them for a year and speak their language as well as our own. If learning the mercy of Jesus Christ can make them treat their enemies less cruelly, it will serve them well," I said, adding, "I only hope I can be as useful to you in this project as my brother-in-law was at Sainte-Marie among the Huron."

"I know Médard well," Father Ragueneau said. "Together we made maps of the country where the Huron lived. His work was excellent, and he went everywhere, soon knowing the land better than anyone. However, as the years passed he began to show a greater interest in the fur trade than in the advancement of Christianity."

"One day, when he's ready to take me, I will go with him to seek new places and new nations."

"If you do I hope you can dissuade him from trading guns. It was his willingness to supply the Algonquin nations with guns that eventually led to disagreements between us. I tried but could not persuade him to refrain from this trade, for your brother-in-law can be an extremely unyielding man."

"So I have been told. As for myself, my only interest is to help the Iroquois who were kind to me in spite of being known for their cruelty."

"Then, my son, we share the same purpose. And I know of no better way to tame the wild instincts of man than to teach him the love and gentleness of Jesus Christ. To this end, it is our fervent hope to establish a mission among them, and from heathens bring forth Christians. Father Simon Le Moyne – who also speaks well of you – has just returned from the south side of Lake Ontario, where the

Onondaga live, with some good news . . . "

"I know their country well," I said. "The Mohawk – who live closest to the Dutch in New Holland – and the Onondaga often visit one another to make plans for war. Moreover, the Onondaga have to pass through Mohawk territory to bring their furs to the Dutch."

"Which seems to be one of the reasons the Onondaga wish to have peace with us. By bringing their furs here they could bypass the Mohawk who now demand a share of their profits. The Onondaga sent word with Father Le Moyne that they are anxious to have us establish a settlement among them and will send ambassadors soon to hear our reply. Since you have been to their country and know their language, we hope you can join us then as an interpreter."

However, the Onondaga did not return later in the summer as expected. As Father Ragueneau told me afterwards, the Mohawk were jealous that Father Le Moyne had gone to see the Onondaga first. They told the French the Iroquois were one house, and that we should begin with the foundation – by which they meant themselves – rather than go down the chimney by which they meant the Onondaga.

As a result, the next summer Father Le Moyne visited the Mohawk, undertaking the journey as a gesture of friendship and to affirm the peace between the Mohawk and ourselves.

Thus, it wasn't until the following September – a month after Simon Le Moyne left for the Mohawk Valley – that a delegation of Onondaga passed through Trois Rivières. Anticipating my role as interpreter, I accompanied them to Québec.

In Québec, a large assembly of French and Onondaga gathered on the grounds outside the walls of Fort St. Louis.

Governor Lauzon sat at the head of the French delegation between Father Joseph Le Mercier, the new Superior of the Canada missions, and Father Paul Ragueneau, his predecessor in that office. I sat next to Father Ragueneau.

The Onondaga sent eighteen ambassadors, and the principal chiefs of the Huron and the Algonquin who lived near Québec were also present.

The gathering – the native chiefs wearing animal skin costumes and with eagle feathers in their hair, and the French, dressed in the black robes of priests; the blue coats and hats of the military; and the regal suits of Governor Lauzon and his officials – was colorful to behold.

Rising to his feet, the chief spokesman for the Onondaga spoke for a long time before coming to the purpose of their visit.

"We have come to invite you to send settlers to

our country," he said, "where they shall be as one people with us as they were when they lived with the Huron.

"We also want the Black Robes to come with them, to instruct our children and to make all our people Christians.

"We are also here to assure you that all the upper Iroquois – the Oneida, the Onondaga, the Cayuga, and the Seneca – are of one mind, being unanimous in our desire to have a sincere peace."

After the Onondaga chief finished, Father Ragueneau rose to speak.

"Brothers," he said, "we are anxious to enter further into your hearts and to lose no time in an affair of such consequence. As a sign of our good faith we are ready to send two of our dear Fathers back with you. They will look for a suitable place to build a chapel, where all your people will be able to come."

The following spring, at the beginning of May, the Onondaga arrived in Québec to hear our decision. Again I joined them on their way through Trois Rivières and on my arrival in the capital went to see Father Ragueneau, prepared to offer my services.

"Is the Governor willing to send the soldiers and settlers the Onondaga asked for?" I asked.

In answer to my question, Father Ragueneau said, "The Governor hesitates to send men who may soon be needed to defend Québec against the Mohawk, who have shown they wish to continue the war with the Huron and the Algonquin. To have their way, they are doing everything they can to destroy our truce with the upper Iroquois.

"Two ambassadors from the Seneca came last November to affirm their desire for peace with the French and our Algonquin allies and to express their desire for Christian instruction, having already seen the good effects it has brought to the Onondaga. The Seneca, as you know, are the largest of the Iroquois nations, and their support of the peace would compel the other Iroquois to honor it."

"When I was there with the Mohawk, it took us three days to cross their land. On the way we passed through many large towns," I said.

"Yes, and the Seneca's participation in the peace must concern the Mohawk, who have profited from their wars with us because it has obliged the upper Iroquois to pass through the lower country in order to trade with the Dutch. This state of affairs has enabled the Mohawk to dominate the others while the nearness of the Dutch has made them the strongest of the Iroquois by having the most guns."

"All the Mohawk have guns," I said, "while the upper Iroquois don't have as many, and the Seneca who are the farthest from New Holland have the fewest."

"That is why we think the Mohawk killed the two Seneca ambassadors as they were returning to tell their countrymen of the peace between the upper Iroquois and us. Their bodies were discovered on the way, scalped and full of wounds. It could only have been the work of the Mohawk whose design seems to be to turn the upper Iroquois against us."

The next day I met with Father Ragueneau again, to learn what the Governor had decided.

"The Governor has considered all sides of the problem and has concluded we must act quickly," Father Ragueneau said. "The Onondaga say if we don't go to their country soon, they will join forces with the Mohawk to destroy us. Monsieur Lauzon is of the opinion we could not withstand such a concerted assault and has therefore decided it is better to risk a small company of men in Onondaga than the entire colony.

"Monsieur Zachary Dupuis, the commander of our soldiers here, is assembling a garrison of men for the new fort and several of our Fathers are preparing to leave with them. Can you accompany them to Montréal past the threat of Mohawk who may be waiting along the way?"

"I would gladly go all the way to Onondaga if I didn't have to wait for Médard's return. We expected him last summer," I said.

Chapter Fourteen
Médard's Precious Cargo

Summer came and passed, with still no sign of Médard. Then, when we had almost given up hope for his safe return, Médard appeared near the end of August. Charles Le Moyne's man and fifty Ottawa canoes carrying two hundred and fifty men and a precious cargo of furs were with him.

Médard and his crew didn't stay long in Trois Rivières as the season was late and two ships from France were waiting in Québec.

"Come with us," Médard said as they prepared to leave.

What a welcome awaited us. As we approached the landing place in lower town cannons boomed from the ramparts of Fort St. Louis above, while inhabitants gathered by the river cheered.

Their enthusiasm was understandable, for the colony had been on the brink of ruin. All the furs the merchants got during the past two years of peace had been lost at sea leaving them and the colony deep in debt. Médard's furs and the ones the Ottawa brought saved both the merchants and New France.

Governor Lauzon received us in front of Fort St. Louis while, on all sides, the citizens applauded. Then, in a gesture of friendship, the Governor and the Ottawa captains exchanged gifts. The Governor had swords for the captains, while they gave him white ermine collars for his coats.

After these ceremonies were over we descended to the King's Stores in lower town to receive payment for our pelts. The Ottawa were paid with guns and ammunition, while Médard's furs were valued at 15,000 French pounds, out of which he had to pay the tax of one quarter, levied to meet the expenses of the colony. For his share of beaver pelts, Charles Le Moyne's man received an equal amount.

For the most part we were satisfied with our transactions, and all the way back to Trois Rivières the Ottawa played with their new guns as if they were toys. They never seemed to tire of loading and firing them, making so much noise that if the Iroquois had been on the river it would have brought them down upon us.

Nevertheless, Médard complained about having to turn over one quarter of his earnings to the Governor. "I saved the colony from ruin and for thanks they took away a quarter of my profits," he said over and over during the months that followed. In spite of his complaints he was a rich man now, even after repaying more than 1,000 pounds to his creditors.

One night, not long after his return, he told me the full extent of his discoveries.

"On the other side of Lake Huron, where the Ottawa and the Ojibway have fled to be far away from the Iroquois, there are many other nations like them that speak the same language as the Algonquin who live near us. Like the Algonquin here, they live by hunting and fishing and don't grow corn as the Huron did," he said.

"They told me there is a people on the north side of Lake Superior who in winter put on coats made of the finest beaver. At the rapids between Lake Huron and Lake Superior we met some of these people, called the Cree, who had come there to trade with the Ottawa.

"Their pelts were the best I have ever seen. The Cree said there are more beaver in their country than anywhere in the world and they invited me to visit them with our merchandise, which they value highly. Because they are afraid of the Iroquois, they won't come to us.

"They said they spend their summers on the shores of a salty sea they reach by following rivers north of Lake Superior. Though they call this sea the Bay of the North, I believe it is the bay the Englishman Henry Hudson discovered.

"If I am right, then this kingdom with the finest store of furs in the world can also be reached by sea. I plan to go back to Lake Superior to discover if what I think is true. When I do we will go together and claim this empire for France, and at the same time make ourselves the richest men in the New World."

At this point – as if to give me time to absorb the significance of what he had just said – Médard paused his exposition. We were sitting on wooden chairs by the fireplace. Then, leaning towards me – with a concerned expression – he said, "Pierre, you must swear to tell no one what I have told you. If anyone else learns what I have discovered, they will try to get there before us."

Chapter Fifteen
Huron Dilemma

The following spring I returned to Québec where Father Ragueneau was making preparations to conduct some of the Huron to Onondaga.

"The Mohawk assault on the Huron on Ile d'Orléans last year has brought about the consequences I feared," he said. "Afterwards the Huron begged the Mohawk for a truce, which they accepted on condition the Huron agree to go with them to live in the Mohawk Valley. This put the Huron in a quandary because the Onondaga had also been promised their share of Huron and last November an army of a hundred Onondaga came ready to take the Huron with them, by force if necessary."

Father Ragueneau was clearly distressed at this turn of events for it was he who brought the remnants of the Huron to live on Ile d'Orléans – ten miles downstream from Québec – after the Iroquois destroyed their homeland ten years ago.

"The poor Huron saw they must either leave and run the risk of being killed in their new country or stay here with the French and be killed by one or other of the Iroquois," he said.

"Finally the three Huron clans – the Cords, the Bears, and the Rocks – decided to go their separate ways. The Cords said they would stay with the

French, the Bears would go live with the Mohawk, and the Rocks said they were willing to go to Onondaga, provided the Black Robes went with them and the Onondaga returned to get them in canoes of peace, and not those of war.

"The Onondaga said they would meet the Rocks in Montréal this spring after the ice is gone. Father Simon Le Moyne is to accompany the Bears to Anihé and I will follow the rest of my children to Onondaga."

"Since Médard is not yet ready to leave for the west, I can go with you," I said.

"I'm glad you can join us. We need good men like you to help with our work in the upper country where the Onondaga live, while at the same time keeping an eye on the movements of all the Iroquois, especially the Mohawk.

"But tell me, Pierre, why do you want to live again with these people who can be so cruel?"

"When I lived in Anihé I saw much that was good in them, and that is the reason I want to help them now," I said.

Chapter Sixteen
Ominous Journey

It was the middle of June when we left Québec in three small ships. Along with twenty Frenchmen, the other passengers were the fifty Christian Huron – twelve of them men, the rest women and children – the Onondaga were coming to Montréal to get.

Besides three Jesuit priests – Father Paul Ragueneau, Father Francois Du Peron, and Brother Louis Boesme – the other Frenchmen were lay helpers – some to serve as housekeepers for the Jesuits and some to act as reinforcements for the soldiers already in Onondaga. As for myself, my main duty was to act as an interpreter for the priests during their missionary work in Onondaga villages.

As we progressed slowly up the broad St. Lawrence River on our way to Montréal, Father Ragueneau shared his hopes for the new mission in Onondaga – now known as Sainte-Marie among the Iroquois – with me. "After we lost Sainte-Marie among the Huron, I prayed to our Lord to grant us another opportunity to carry His Word to the heathen. Now, in a fitting irony, he is leading us to save the savage souls of the Iroquois who destroyed it," he said.

"Your mission among the Huron was before my time, but Médard told me it was our diseases and the guns the Iroquois had that were the cause of their destruction," I said.

"Your brother-in-law was wrong," Father Ragueneau said. "It was God's punishment to those Huron who refused to accept the Blood of Christ, choosing instead to remain heathens. The proof is, God showed His mercy to the five hundred Christian Huron who found refuge with us in Québec."

When we arrived in Montréal a few days later, the Onondaga who were to conduct us to their country had not arrived. Without them we dared not continue, since we didn't know the way and needed their help to go around the many dangerous rapids above Montréal, the last French settlement west of Québec.

Finally, about two weeks later, we saw them coming around a point at the bottom of the Saint Louis rapids, about three miles from the fort. When we saw them stop and go ashore before reaching us, we wondered why.

"Perhaps they are preparing their speeches for when they meet us," Father Ragueneau said. However, as we later discovered, their real reason was far more sinister.

After the thirty Onondaga and fifteen Seneca with them had landed, they told us that seven of the Seneca had drowned coming down the rapids, and that this had been the reason they went ashore. Then, according to tradition, we exchanged gifts along with professions of friendship.

Following these ceremonies the Onondaga captain addressed his Huron counterpart. "Do not be afraid," he said. "For we no longer think of you as our enemy, but now regard you as our cousins. You will adore our country, which soon shall be yours too. But, if you doubt my word, please accept this wampum necklace as a peace offering."

The captain of the Christian Huron took the necklace and said, "We are not afraid as it is God's will that brings us to your country, where it is better to die peacefully with our brothers than to remain beside the French and be murdered. For us it is better to live with the Iroquois than to go to war against them and be burned. Women, prepare our baggage that we may soon depart."

But it was another week before we could go. The reason for the delay was we needed new transportation as the eleven Iroquois canoes would not suffice to carry us all, and the boats we left Québec in could go no farther because of the rapids that lay ahead. Finally, we found another twenty canoes, these ones Algonquin-made, lighter, stronger and bigger than the Iroquois ones, and each able to carry seven men.

The first day of the voyage to Onondaga was slow and arduous. The Jesuits had brought so much baggage with them that the canoes were in danger of capsizing, especially if a wind had come up. When we got to the St. Louis rapids, a short distance from Montréal, those of us who had to carry their baggage around the rapids were none too happy about it.

While the rest of us – Frenchmen, Huron, and Iroquois, alike – grumbled and struggled with their things, the clerics in their long black cassocks waited at the other end to supervise the loading of the canoes. As we stowed their belongings Father Ragueneau fretted. "Mind the holy chalices and incense burners – and be sure not to spill any of our precious holy water. It was blessed in Rome by the Father General, himself – it's irreplaceable . . . No, no, no, put the mass kits here, in the middle, where they won't get wet," he said, watching while surly Iroquois roughly handled the scores of holy relics the Jesuits used in their trade.

After completing the portage we continued for another ten miles or so, stopping for the night where the St. Lawrence broadens into Lake St. Louis.

The next morning, before continuing on our way, the Iroquois threw the Fathers' bundles on the ground. "We are no longer willing to look after these useless things," the Iroquois captain said.

But Father Ragueneau was not about to give up his sacred cargo easily. Nevertheless, although he tried hard to persuade the Iroquois to put them back in the canoes, they remained adamant. "It's enough that we bring you to our country without having to carry so many useless articles as well," their captain said.

Finally, after a heated dispute, Father Ragueneau yielded to the stronger side and instructed Father Du Peron to remain with the baggage until more canoes could be brought up from Montréal.

All but seven of our twenty Frenchmen stayed behind with Father Du Peron. As we prepared to leave, the Iroquois treated Father Ragueneau coldly, and he had difficulty finding someone who would take him. Finally, he persuaded two of the Iroquois to take him and Brother Louis Boesme along with two of the other Frenchmen.

For some time afterwards our journey proceeded without further incident. At the end of Lake St. Louis, we arrived at the junction of the two great rivers of Canada, where the cold and dark Ottawa River, descending from the northeast, merges with the warm and clear St. Lawrence River coming from the southwest. We continued on the St. Lawrence and by-passed two more steep and violent rapids, our portages made easier without the burden of the Fathers' baggage. Three days after leaving Montréal, we came to another enlargement of the river, called Lake St. Francis by the French.

It was a shallow clear lake, beautiful to behold with a mountain range on the south side, pale blue in the distance, and wooded plains on the north, where we stopped to hunt and fish. Among the rushes along the shore, we killed several moose and scores of ducks without even leaving our boats. Others formed hunting parties to go into the woods to shoot deer. We speared hundreds of fish, as well. We remained on Lake St. Francis for several days, eating well while putting aside fresh meat and fish for the journey ahead.

We were still on the lake when one morning, as we were setting out, four Huron men with two women fell behind. Before the rest of us noticed they weren't keeping up, we heard them singing a farewell song; then watched in astonishment as they turned their canoe around and headed back towards Montréal.

Although their departure infuriated the Iroquois, they made no move to stop the six Huron from leaving. But the next morning we got a hint of the treacherous plot they had been secretly hatching since their arrival in Montréal.

First, the Seneca left before daybreak on the pretext of leaving for the war against the Erie. As they departed their terrifying war cries pierced the dawn stillness, sending chills up and down our spines.

Then, before the rest of us could embark, the Onondaga made sure no more Huron could escape by making them go with them. At the same time they made the seven remaining Frenchmen ride in separate canoes. Outnumbered, and with two or three guards in every canoe, we dared not resist.

We stopped for the night on a large island at the end of Lake St. Francis where the river began to narrow again. There, the Onondaga captain persuaded the Huron to make camp at the top of a hill, about forty yards from where the Onondaga were setting up their own. We French also retired to put up our shelters, some distance from the others. When we had finished I set out to visit the Huron.

As I walked along the water's edge on my way there, I saw a band of Iroquois hidden in the woods wearing war paint. Disguised though they were, they appeared to be the Seneca who earlier that morning were supposed to have left to fight the Erie. Alarmed at this discovery, I hurried to the Huron camp, where I found Father Ragueneau with his Christian charges.

Nearby, the Onondaga captain sat next to the Christian Huron captain, who was renowned far and wide for his valor, having killed many Iroquois in his time. The Onondaga captain had come to assure his counterpart he had nothing to fear.

"Brother," he said, "cheer up. You shall not be killed by dogs, for you are a man and a captain in war, as I myself am. Before any other can kill you I will die in your defense."

Just then, blood curdling shrieks pierced the air as the Seneca warriors – for it was indeed the same ones who had pretended to leave for the war with the Erie – rushed from their hiding place and fell upon the Huron men with their knives, hatchets, and swords. At that same moment, the captain of the Onondaga grabbed the medal of the Blessed Virgin that hung by a chain from the Huron captain's neck, and said, "No, brother, you shall be killed by no other hand than mine!"

The Huron captain, seeing himself betrayed, pulled free of the Iroquois captain who was left holding the sacred medal in his clenched fist. At the same time one of the Seneca swooped down on the Huron captain who, unholstering the hatchet hanging by his side, killed his last Iroquois before he himself was cut to pieces. When the carnage had ended, the Iroquois threw the bodies of the Christian Huron men into the river.

Presently, the Iroquois brought the Huron women together. The women stood in silence, their eyes cast down upon the ground, while their husbands' murderers told them not to be afraid for they would not be killed. Then, after stripping them of their belongings, the Iroquois let them go.

While I stood by, admiring the stoicism of these women who had just witnessed their husbands' brutal massacre, Father Ragueneau tried to console them. "Remember, my children," he said, "God did not promise Christians joy for this life but for eternity; it is by patiently suffering our miseries on earth that we shall be happy in heaven."

As the sun descended over the river, some Iroquois arrived to summon Father Ragueneau to a council. Here he learned the extraordinary reasons for the slaughter that had taken place only a couple of hours before. After the council had ended, Father Ragueneau returned to fetch his dish and to tell us we were all invited to join the Iroquois in a feast of friendship.

He found five of us – only Brother Boesme had refused to participate – with our weapons ready, having convinced ourselves in his absence that the meeting with the Iroquois was meant to prepare our own deaths. The two Iroquois captains who had escorted Father Ragueneau back to our camp saw our agitation and cocked their guns.

"There is nothing to fear," the Onondaga captain said. "We wish only to be your friends and your brothers."

"You are our bosom companions and our brothers," the Seneca captain with him said. "Lay your arms aside and join us at the feast of friendship."

But the four other Frenchmen who didn't understand the Iroquois language were excited and ready to fight to the last man.

"Calm yourselves, my children," Father Ragueneau said. "The Iroquois intend us no harm. The carnage is finished. The council was to let me know the reason our seven Christian Huron men were killed. From the Seneca I learned it was to avenge the death of their seven comrades who drowned in the St. Louis rapids. To their way of thinking, it was our fault since they were on their way to fetch us and the Christian Huron when the accident occurred. However, I have been assured we have nothing more to fear. The lives of the Huron men are sufficient retribution for us all. Now let us put this tragedy behind us and go to their banquet as a gesture of goodwill."

I picked up my dish and returned with Father Ragueneau to the Iroquois camp. After we had eaten, Father Ragueneau asked the Seneca captain to lend him three necklaces of wampum.

Then he stood up and threw one of them into the middle of the assembly, saying, "The first gift is to preserve the friendship between the French and the upper Iroquois. Bury your hatchets, for too much innocent blood has already been spilled. God has seen it, and if you continue with your cruelties, He will become angry and take revenge upon those who are the cause of it."

The Iroquois responded with a chorus of "ho, ho's," which signified their approval of what he said.

Only the Onondaga captain was unrepentant. "It was your big chief, himself, and the chief of the Black Robes who gave us permission to kill those dogs," he said, meaning the Governor of New

France and Father Joseph Le Mercier, Superior of the Canada missions.

"That is false," Father Ragueneau said. "Such betrayals are as far from our spirit as heaven is from earth."

"Well, you do not know all that I know," the captain said, finally.

Resuming his address, Father Ragueneau threw down the second necklace. "This is to encourage you to treat the poor Huron women and children kindly, no longer considering them as a nation apart but as one people with you," he said. The Iroquois agreed to this proposal in the same manner as the first.

"The third is for us to continue our voyage as though nothing had happened. To this end we ask you to conduct us safely to your country, and to take care that our baggage is not left behind and does not become wet," Father Ragueneau said after throwing the last necklace onto the ground.

After Father Ragueneau had finished, the Iroquois captains instructed their men to take care of our merchandise and to render an account of it upon our arrival in Onondaga. Everyone then retired to their places for the night. It was pitiful to see the poor Huron women, holding their children close, return to the shelters their unfortunate husbands made for them. Hoping the worst was over, we French made our beds, too, though we slept with our arms by our sides and maintained a watch throughout the night.

Finally, after a long and arduous passage up the St. Lawrence River we followed the shore on the south side of Lake Ontario to a small river, called the Oswego by the Iroquois, which originated in the land of the Onondaga. We followed this river, which had a strong current and many dangerous rapids, to a smaller one that drained a small lake, where the year before Commander Dupuis and his party had erected the fort and mission of Sainte-Marie among the Iroquois. The river was six miles long and the lake, called Lake Onondaga, fifteen around. Here we found a countryside that was pleasant to behold, for both its beauty and its abundance.

At last we came to the landing place at the foot of the fort and mission of Sainte-Marie among the Iroquois. The fort and mission was impressive looking and well made. There were four log buildings, two larger ones and two smaller ones. An inner and an outer palisade with two bastions in opposite corners enclosed the compound, making it impregnable to the Iroquois. In a large clearing surrounding the fort the men who preceded us raised wheat for our French bread. It grew well here, and covered more than a square mile of land.

For some dozen miles around, the country was as smooth as a board. On all sides there were fields of corn, pumpkins, and French turnips. Nearby there were trees with chestnuts and walnuts, as well as an abundance of fruit. There were also a great many hogs, so fat they could barely move, and plenty of fowl of all kinds, and wild pigeons so numerous that seven or eight hundred might be taken in nets at one time. So, to our way of thinking, this was not a wild country, but abundant in everything.

The reverend Fathers who had come the year before along with some forty other Frenchmen, domestics and volunteers alike, received us warmly. We began to recount our adventures, having thought never to see one another again, and being delighted to have been mistaken.

Chapter Seventeen
Sainte-Marie among the Iroquois

Onondaga, Iroquois Territory – 1657-1658

Not long after our arrival I accompanied Father Ragueneau to one of the Onondaga villages near the fort, where we had the first hint of the Iroquois' malevolent designs.

First, we learned the Erie, their enemy to the west, had been conquered. Then one of the elders, who seemed favorably disposed to Christianity, said, "As soon as the rest of the Huron have been brought from Québec, the war with the French will resume. Fifty of our men are there now to persuade the remaining Huron to join their relatives already here."

Later, we learned those fifty Onondaga turned out to be our salvation. Warned by Father Du Peron and the six Huron who had left our expedition and returned to Québec before our arrival in Onondaga, the Huron put their suitors off until spring. This forced the Onondaga, and some Mohawk, there for the same purpose, to spend the winter in the vicinity of Québec, where they waited for spring to bring the rest of the Huron to their country.

During this time a small company of Oneida descended upon Montréal and killed three of our countrymen who, having placed their trust in the false peace, were working in fields far outside the walls of the fort. In a sign of war, the Oneida returned to their villages carrying the three French scalps on the ends of sticks.

As soon as he heard of this treacherous act, Monsieur Louis d'Ailleboust, the acting Governor of New France, dispatched orders to the commanders at Montréal and Trois Rivières to arrest any Iroquois then present in the French colony. Before long, twelve of them, Mohawk as well as Onondaga, were rounded up and delivered in irons to Québec, where the Governor promised to hold them as hostages until the French ensnared in Iroquois territory were returned unharmed.

From informants we learned the Mohawk, upon hearing this, held a council at which they vowed to unleash a new and unrelenting war against the French as soon as they could obtain the release of their imprisoned comrades.

The first signs of war came in early February when an Iroquois army began assembling at Onondaga. Two hundred Mohawk warriors from the lower country joined forces with forty Oneida and more troops of Onondaga, Cayuga and Seneca.

Daily they met to celebrate the call to arms with songs and banquets.

A council of the five nations of the Iroquois Confederacy was summoned. Again Providence aided us in the form of another old man who had fallen sick and wished to be baptized before passing on to the other world. He told us the council had resolved that, when the ice in Lake Ontario was gone and the war resumed, the first to feel their wrath would be ourselves, the French trapped in Onondaga. Only the hostages the Governor held prevented the Iroquois from immediately executing the first step of their evil plan.

Seeing the mission was doomed our Fathers and Monsieur Dupuis, the commander of the fort, met to decide what to do. Their conclusion was that we should all leave together and make two boats for our escape.

Though it made us sad to think of leaving such a delightful country, our carpenters set to work, first cutting enough pine boards to make two wide and shallow-draft boats. To make them maneuverable in the rapids, they were pointed at both ends. Each was capable of carrying fourteen or fifteen men as well as fifteen or sixteen hundred pounds of freight. Besides these two boats we had four Algonquin-style canoes and four Iroquois ones, altogether enough to carry our party of fifty-three Frenchmen.

To conceal them from the Iroquois we made a false ceiling in the building where we planned to make them. We worked on the boats at night and during the day stored them in the attic above, confident the Iroquois – who were unfamiliar with our methods of construction – would suspect nothing.

As winter came to an end, with the two boats ready, we began to think of a way to escape their clutches. Our main problem was to get away without being noticed. But we couldn't move all our boats, canoes, and equipment without making a lot of noise. Yet, unless we got away without the Iroquois being aware of it there was no hope of escape. For if they had the least suspicion we intended to depart our wholesale destruction would be assured.

Monsieur Dupuis and the Jesuit Fathers met several times, trying to think of a way to get away without being heard. When they failed to come up with a plan Father Ragueneau came to me. "Perhaps you can think of something," he said. "You've lived with them and know their habits better than anyone."

Easter was coming, and it gave me an idea. I took my plan to Father Ragueneau and Monsieur Dupuis. "We'll tell them a day is approaching when we are accustomed to treat our friends with food and entertainment. They understand such celebrations, so I am sure they'll believe us," I said.

"It sounds like a good plan, but how do we avoid alerting them when we begin loading the boats," Father Ragueneau said.

"Another thing I learned from the Iroquois is, it is considered bad manners not to eat everything put in front of you. Knowing this we can keep serving them new courses until they are so stuffed they fall into a stupor. In such a state they won't hear a thing."

"Young fellow, not only do I think this plan of yours could work," Monsieur Dupuis said, "it will challenge our ingenuity to carry it out. I'll order my cooks to begin preparing for your banquet right away. But how will we let them know about it?"

"Since many of the Onondaga remember me from when I was here with the Mohawk, let me tell them," I said.

Not long after, I met with some of the captains I got to know when I was with the Mohawk. I told them about the feast day coming up when it was our tradition to feed and entertain our friends. Then I said, "Having no greater friends than yourselves, everyone is invited to this great celebration."

"We will gladly come," said one, "both to become acquainted with your customs and to fill our bellies."

On the day of the festivity our guests began to arrive. For having concocted this plan and being known to the Onondaga, Monsieur Dupuis made me the official host.

"Sing and eat to your heart's content," I said to each new arrival.

Throughout the afternoon we entertained them

with plays and dances, and even performed magic tricks to hold their attention.

All day we allowed no one to enter the fort. "It is our practice," I said to those who asked why, "not to reveal the splendor of our banquets before presenting them at the table."

Having beforehand rehearsed these activities among ourselves, we devised contests to see who could make the loudest cries, distributing presents to the ones who made the most noise.

Everyone took part in the festivities. The French sang and danced like the Iroquois and they, to please us, sang and danced our way.

In the meantime, inside the fort, our men prepared bundles of provisions, merchandise, household things, and guns to take with us. For the journey our cooks made excellent biscuits from last year's wheat, and neither did we forget meat from the hogs we kept that had grown fat.

Evening arrived and the guests were invited to take their places on the ground next to the fort where bonfires blazed.

At last the gates to the fort swung open and sentries blew their trumpets. The banquet was about to begin. To give themselves a better appetite our excited guests shouted and clapped their hands, and danced all around.

For appetizers, two dozen men emerged from the fort carrying between them a dozen large kettles full of beaten corn mixed with a kind of mincemeat made from finely chopped nuts, dried fruit, and bear fat. While servers were busy filling the guests' bowls, the most venerable of the elders rose to speak.

"Long shall we remember this day," he said. "Our children and their children after them will speak of it with wonder, saying never before was such a magnificent banquet seen. To commemorate this memorable occasion, let us give thanks to the Great Spirit who has seen fit to bring among us such generous men as the French who honor us so."

Then the feast began in earnest. The Iroquois ate like a pack of wolves, with eyes bigger than their stomachs. Their manners were impeccable. Except for a chorus of slurps and the rhythmic scraping sound their spoons made in wooden bowls, they made not a sound.

First two kettles full of ducks arrived; then two full of turtles. The guests showed their appreciation with whoops of delight. And no sooner had they finished one dish than another sort arrived. This one a broth of fish, eels, salmon, and carp, which renewed their appetites.

As the evening wore on – sure no one would leave their place – we entertained them with songs and dances to prevent them from falling asleep.

But the banquet wasn't over yet. A kettle of venison in corn flour thickened with bear oil came next. Some of the guests beat their bellies, some shook their heads, while others stopped their mouths to keep in what they had eaten.

They showed their appreciation, making strange faces and rolling their eyes up and down. "Enjoy yourselves," I said to some of the Onondaga I knew, "for it is customary for us to make a fuss over our friends."

Meanwhile we, the hosts, had not eaten. It is our way, we told them.

As the end of the festivities drew near, nothing was spared that could add to the confusion. When our men inside the fort began carrying our things out to the docks – to hide the sound of their movements – we competed with one other to see who could make the most noise.

But all good things must come to an end. The hour to depart had arrived, for everything was embarked. The Iroquois could hold out no longer. They told us they must sleep. "Enough, we can take no more," some said.

I said the French were weary as well, and would also sleep a while.

Before leaving, to bid them farewell and to help them dream, I got out my guitar and sang a French lullaby I made especially for them:

Sleep dear friends with bellies full,

Though we hate to leave your country so fair
Where luscious fruits grow everywhere
We must cross Lake Ontario
To our land of ice and snow

We wished to be your friends
But you would not make amends
And now we must go away so far
Because we like our scalps just where they are

So, with regret, we must separate
Not as friends, but with hate

Adieu, Adieu, Adieu

Then, not wishing to disturb our guests, we crept away without saying goodbye. All was quiet, the only sound the contented snoring of the Iroquois beside dying fires. We shut the fort up as if we were in it, then left quietly by the back door. In silence, we embarked. Then pushed away from shore into the darkness.

As we left Sainte-Marie among the Iroquois, we all felt sad. We had had such high hopes, especially Father Ragueneau. But there was no time for regrets as we made our way towards the river that would take us out of Lake Onondaga. The going was difficult because, even though it was the beginning of spring, the lake still froze over every night. By the time we reached the middle, ice was forming so fast we feared our boats would get stuck in it.

As we neared the end of the lake, the ice had become so thick we had to use poles to break a passage. Progress was slow and difficult. Finally, at daybreak, we came within sight of the entrance to the outlet, where there was no more ice. If the Iroquois had looked out then, they would have seen us, but as we reached open water we leaned into our oars and soon put ourselves beyond that danger. We continued on throughout the day, with the strength only fear can give, stopping neither to rest nor to eat. We followed the little river out of Lake Onondaga and entered the Oswego that descended to Lake Ontario, where we had to keep a sharp lookout for rocks and several uncharted precipices along the way.

Ten days after our departure from Onondaga, we came to the beginning of the St. Lawrence River, where we encountered new difficulties. Because of the many islands around it, the entrance to the river was difficult to find but, after going back and forth many times, we finally found the main channel.

For the next two days we proceeded without danger. Then, as we entered a colder country, navigation became more and more difficult. The section of the river with the most dangerous rapids was littered with large islands of ice and snow, all packed together, that made tremendous noises whenever they shifted. Often we had to use our axes to break through the ice. All around, the land was covered in snow.

Then, without warning, and before we could stop ourselves, we were pulled into a gigantic chute. A rushing torrent propelled us helplessly forward towards huge boulders that threw up mountains of water. If we hadn't used our oars and paddles to get around them we would have been smashed to pieces. With icy water pouring into our boats and the frantic cries of men barely audible above the thundering roar of the river, we were like the crew of a ship at sea caught in a storm. The violence of the current drove us onwards through enormous rapids, which we would never have willingly gone down.

Our fears redoubled when we saw one of the canoes with four of our men overturn at the bottom of a ledge that spanned the river. With no detour around it we all had to go over it. Three of them drowned as they tried to swim to shore, but the one who could not swim was saved by clinging to his boat. At the bottom of the rapids we picked him out of the water half frozen and ready to let go out of weakness. It was fortunate the river was swollen, or none of us would have escaped such a powerful flood of water.

A few nights later as we neared the end of our journey, we saw fires on the south shore of the river. Afraid they belonged to the Iroquois, we descended the St. Louis rapids in the middle of the night, trusting in the depth of the water at this time of year to get through safely. Later, we were told that if we had arrived only the day before we could not possibly have made it, for the river below the rapids was then covered with ice. We would have been unable to turn back, and the current would have swept us under the ice to our end. It was our good fortune to come after the ice had melted.

It was still dark when we arrived at the gates of Montréal, where we were challenged by startled sentries, who thought we might be the Iroquois. The French received us like long lost relatives returned from the dead, and we thanked God for our deliverance.

Here we learned the Iroquois were already on the warpath and two hundred Mohawk had been seen in the vicinity. The enemy was also at Trois Rivières and Québec, where they had taken prisoners and killed some of our Algonquin allies.

The war with the Iroquois had resumed, and not even the Jesuits could hold out any hope for peace with such a treacherous nation.

After we had rested in Montréal for two weeks, which we had been unable to do on the long and dangerous journey back, we continued on to Trois Rivières where most of us lived.

Chapter Eighteen
Preparing To Meet The Cree

When I got back from Onondaga, Médard was making preparations to go to the Bay of the North.

"It is time to visit the Cree who have promised to meet us at the west end of Lake Superior," he said. "Because of many swift and dangerous rivers along the way, getting there will be difficult. And when we finally arrive we will have to stay the winter, which will be long and bitterly cold."

"No rapids could be more treacherous than the ones on the St. Lawrence River we came down after our escape from Onondaga," I said.

"That is true, but the greatest threat will come from the Iroquois, who patrol the river constantly and will do everything they can to stop us," Médard said.

"And now that the entire Iroquois Confederacy are united to destroy us, they are more dangerous than ever. I witnessed their preparations for war in Onondaga."

"Precisely, and because of all your experience there is no one more suitable than you, Pierre, to join me on this great adventure. You are young, strong, courageous and intelligent, and having twice escaped the Iroquois, you will be an inspiration to our Algonquin allies. If this voyage appeals to you, there is no one I would rather have go with me."

"I agree with you; I know the Iroquois better than anyone. And, because they betrayed us in Onondaga and have killed my friends and relatives, if we should meet up with them I will revenge myself upon them. I once loved them dearly but since their treachery in Onondaga I no longer care what becomes of them. Nor is there anything I would rather do than go with you and make new discoveries. When do we leave?"

"Soon, Pierre."

But we did not leave shortly after all. That summer the Iroquois attacks were so ferocious we had to remain in Trois Rivières another year.

Finally, as ice began to form in the St. Lawrence River, the enemy retreated and we prepared for our great voyage in search of the Bay of the North.

We chose our freight with care. Though we would be away at least a year – perhaps two – we kept our necessities to a minimum. A barrel of salt pork and some sacks of cornmeal were all the provisions we planned to take. For meat, we intended to live off the land.

The rest of our cargo was made up of the things we needed to trade with the Cree for their beaver pelts. Over the winter we accumulated all manner of iron utensils, carefully packing dozens of knives, axes, awls, needles, fishhooks, and kettles for the journey.

One day, as we were taking stock of our merchandise, Médard said, "These are things the natives value. Such simple metal implements as these have the power to transform their existence. As soon as they have them, they discard their old tools of bone and stone.

"Consider how much easier it is to fell a tree with an iron axe than to bring it down by burning through it. Or how more convenient it is to cook your supper in a copper pot than in a bark vessel with heated stones.

"All our metal tools improve their lives. Which is why they like us so much and bring us their furs. Mostly, though, they want our guns. With them, they can hunt animals with ease as well as defend themselves against the Iroquois."

"The Iroquois get all these things from the Dutch, and guns too," I said. "When we went to war against the Erie they had nothing to defend themselves with except stone-tipped arrows and spears, which made them easy to overcome."

"Which is the reason I have been helping the Algonquin speaking nations get guns. With these they are able to defend themselves and help us defeat the Iroquois," Médard said.

Then pausing to scoop up handfuls of rings, bells, mirrors and combs from a chest full of such things, letting them run through his fingers like Spanish treasure, he said, "Neither must we forget to bring baubles like these for the amusement of their women and children."

Aside from these provisions, all we lacked for the journey was rugged and warm clothing. And no clothes were more suited for the wilderness than those made from the hides of wild animals.

Nor were there any better tailors than the Algonquin women who lived near our fort. A short time after we gave them our order they returned with two new suits of neatly made moose hide jackets and trousers, with leather fringes sewn along the seams, as well as several pairs of moccasins, beautifully ornamented with dyed porcupine quills.

Summer arrived, and after word reached us that traders from the Algonquin nations in the west would come later in the summer we got ready to leave on our great adventure. When they returned to the upper lakes – Lake Huron and Lake Superior – we planned to go with them.

Though apprehensive because of the dangers we would face, Marguérite was also worried about meeting household expenses as Médard's extravagant spending in the three years since his last voyage had nearly drained our resources.

"Must you go so far and risk your lives when so many Iroquois are about," she said one night as we sat around the kitchen table discussing our plans.

"Don't worry Marguérite," Médard said. "The fur trade is the quickest way to repair our fortunes, and with Pierre at my side we'll be safe."

However, before we could leave we required the Governor's permission, since no journey to the interior could be undertaken without it.

But, because of all we had done for the country, we were confident he would grant it.

Chapter Nineteen
The Governor's Conditions

Québec, New France – 1659

Near the end of June we made our way to the capital to seek the permit we needed for our voyage to the west.

From the river's edge in lower town we made our way up Côte de la Montagne, the cinder-covered steep and twisting road Champlain built to the plains above. As we approached the soaring towers of Fort St. Louis with the Governor's residence, Chateau St. Louis, next to it, I became apprehensive.

"I have heard the Jesuits say Monsieur D'Argenson can be difficult. They say he and the new bishop, Monseigneur Laval, have already disagreed over their seating arrangements at mass. You don't think he might turn us down, do you?"

"After all we've done for the country, he wouldn't dare. Don't worry, little brother. He can't refuse us," Médard said.

At Chateau St. Louis a serious looking young man in a black satin suit ushered us into his master's quarters. Governor D'Argenson, who had only taken up his post the year before, emerged from behind a polished mahogany desk to greet us.

"Ah, Sieur des Groseilliers, how happy I am to

meet you. I have heard much about you and your daring young brother-in-law. Here, gentlemen, please be seated."

The Governor, who flattered Médard by using the small title of which he was exceedingly proud, directed us to two upholstered chairs on the side of the desk opposite his.

His appearance was striking. He wore a white silk shirt with cuffs and collar embroidered with lace under a bright gold satin jacket, and had a swath of white silk wound around his waist that held up a pair of royal blue silk pantaloons tucked inside a pair of soft black leather boots reaching above his knees.

We had heard he suffered from ill health but his elegant wardrobe and youth – he was then thirty-three – set off with a waxed moustache and long wavy dark brown hair gave him a dashing appearance.

Still, I thought Médard and I, in our tailored native suits, were just as stylish.

A blazing fire in a large open fireplace gave the spacious apartment a friendly and cozy atmosphere. The cheerfulness of the room and the Governor's warm reception made us feel at ease.

Having exchanged civilities, Médard set out to gain the Governor's approval for our expedition. "With your permission I would like to go over our plan. May I," he said, taking some maps he had with him to a work table nearby.

"Yes, of course," the Governor said, and we all gathered around the table where Médard opened one of his maps.

"Whereas – before the Iroquois drove them away – we used to trade with the Algonquin speaking nations who lived along the eastern shore," he said, pointing to Lake Huron, "farther northwest there is a much larger body of fresh water we call Lake Superior."

"On my last journey I went here," Médard said, moving his finger to the upper corner of Lake Huron, "where these two bodies of water meet . . . "

"Your charts are very well drawn," the Governor said. "We should have copies made."

"You can have these; I have duplicates. As I was about to say, it was here, at the rapids between Lake Huron and Lake Superior, that we met up with the Ottawa – an Algonquin speaking nation who, after fleeing the Iroquois, presently live west of Lake Huron on the south side of Lake Superior – and discovered they got their furs from a peaceable nation called the Cree.

"I befriended some of the Cree, there to trade with the Ottawa, and they promised to show me their country on the north side of Lake Superior, which they say is the richest store house of the best quality beaver anywhere. My plan is to go to Lake Superior and make arrangements with them that will guarantee New France an endless supply of pelts."

Having finished his presentation, Médard – looking pleased with himself – stepped away from the chart table, while he waited for the Governor's response.

"Gentlemen," Monsieur D'Argenson said, after a long pause, "since becoming Governor it has become clear to me that the last thing we need in this country is more fur peddlers. As it is, the settlers have diluted the commerce to such an extent they barely receive enough pelts to cover the costs of their merchandise. In short, the fur trade today is simply not a profitable proposition."

"What you say about the settlers is true," Médard said, maintaining his calm despite the Governor's provocative assertion, "but that is because they don't know how to go about this business, which certainly is not the case with me. The inhabitants of Québec hardly dare go more than two day's journey from here, to Tadoussac at the mouth of the Saguenay River, where the local Algonquin take advantage of their laziness and sell to the highest bidder. But where I go – where no one else dares venture – the natives give me their furs."

"Give them to you? Really, Monsieur, and why do they do that?"

Since the Governor obviously did not understand the way the natives thought, Médard explained.

"Because they love us," he said, simply. Though the Governor appeared incredulous, he didn't pursue the point.

"In any case, there are larger issues to be considered," he said. "Besieged as we are by the Iroquois, if everyone was to do as you, who would be left to defend the colony? No, gentlemen, it is not fur traders we need to make New France prosperous and secure, it is farmers."

"Well, I am no farmer," Médard said. "Since arriving in this country nearly twenty years ago I have been exclusively engaged in the fur trade. First with the Jesuits at Sainte-Marie among the Huron, then later as an independent trader. And, I might add, always to the great benefit of the country."

"Nevertheless, I have proposed to the King that the fur trade be strictly regulated. In the future only those with a permit from me shall be allowed to trade."

"Are you saying you mean to deny us this permit," Médard said, fixing the Governor with a penetrating gaze.

Looking uneasy, the Governor retreated behind his desk and sat down before answering. "No, not necessarily. Not if you agree to my conditions," he said.

"And what are these conditions?" Médard asked, having also taken his chair.

His face turning red, the Governor spoke quickly, "Take two of my men with you, agree to share half the profits with them. Then the permit shall be yours."

Except for the fire crackling in the hearth, the room was silent. For awhile Médard sat staring at Governor D'Argenson. Then, rising to his full height, he leaned so far across the desk his face almost touched that of the Governor, who shrank back in his chair.

"Monsieur," Médard began, slowly and deliberately, "permit me to remind you that it was I who went to the western nations and brought back their furs when because of the Iroquois they were afraid to come to us. It was I who filled the warehouses of New France when the colony was on the brink of ruin. No one else, before or since, has had the courage to do what I have done. And now you ask me to take along two of your servants on another such voyage. Inexperienced men who will only be a danger to themselves and a hindrance to us. No, Monsieur, you cannot expect me to take such risks."

Then, straightening up, he continued in a mocking tone, "And as for dividing our profits with you? Now that is something we will gladly do if in place of your subordinates you will only honor us with your company. For we are both masters and your humble servants," he said, concluding with a sweeping and exaggerated bow.

The Governor was much taken aback. Then, having recovered a little of his composure, he said, "Very well gentlemen, if you refuse my offer, which – considering I am not obliged to make it – is very generous, then you may not leave for the west country.

"Without my permission, you cannot trade. That is the law. If you leave without it you will suffer the consequences upon your return. Now, think that over before you act too hastily."

Without hesitation Médard answered. "Keep your permit," he said. "This country belongs to discoverers not governors, and we know which we are. Come Pierre, we leave immediately for Trois Rivières. Good day, Monsieur."

Half expecting to be arrested for our impudence, we hurried past the guards on our way out. Once away from the fort, relieved to be free of the Governor's machinations, we began to shout over and over for all to hear, "Keep the fur trade free," and, "Discoverers before Governors!"

Chapter Twenty
Jesuit Schemes

Following our disappointing meeting at Château St. Louis, I persuaded Médard to pay a visit to the Jesuits, who I hoped might help us reconcile our differences with the Governor.

The residence and seminary of the Jesuits being only a short distance from the Governor's manor we soon found ourselves inside the hushed corridors of the college where young boys came for as good an education as they could get in France.

While we waited I was struck by the contrast between the Jesuits' austere surroundings and the Governor's opulent quarters. Theirs, with plain domestically made pine tables and chairs; his with imported and polished tables and desks, and upholstered chairs; the windows of the seminary bare; those of the manor covered with blue satin drapes fringed with golden tassels. Crucifixes on their walls, while his were adorned with weapons and shiny armor, and tapestries decorated with hunting scenes.

But behind their simple facade the Jesuits had influenced the direction of New France for three decades. And no one had been more active or intelligent in determining that policy than the former Superior of the Huron mission and former Superior of the Canada Missions who appeared before us like an apparition. Father Paul Ragueneau greeted us warmly.

"Ah, Médard, my old protégé, and young Pierre, the architect of our famous escape from Onondaga. How good to see you both again."

"It's good to see you too, Father," Médard said, with deference in contrast to his recent rudeness towards the Governor.

"I hope you will excuse me for making you wait but I have just returned from teaching philosophy to a class of novitiates. It never ceases to amaze me the difficulty our new recruits seem to have with Aristotelian logic. But I am sure two adventurers like yourselves have not come all this way to hear my views of philosophy."

"You are right," Médard said, and then proceeded to give Father Ragueneau an account of our difficulties with the Governor.

"I don't know how we can help," Father Ragueneau said after listening to our story. "Since our setbacks at our missions among the Huron and the Iroquois, our influence has greatly diminished. Especially with the present Governor who supports the Sulpicians at Montréal over the Company Of Jesus. I'm afraid Monsieur D'Argenson is not our friend.

"These administrators from France," he went on, "do not seem to understand our adopted country. Which is why in the past we sought to assist them with our advice. But this new Governor will not listen to us."

"Nor to me. When I pointed out the benefits our voyage would bring he said, what the country needs is farmers not fur traders and explorers like ourselves," Médard said.

"Well, let us hope someday one of our native sons becomes Governor. Someone like you Médard or Pierre Boucher or Charles Le Moyne. Men who were with me at Sainte-Marie among the Huron. All prominent citizens now, and seigneurs too."

"At least we would work for the betterment of the country unlike these French aristocrats who come here to advance their interests in France," Médard said.

"Yes, Médard, we have lived through some momentous times together. I remember when you came to us as a young man, and we were building the Huron mission. What great hopes we had until the Iroquois forced us to retreat to Québec."

"It was a massacre," Médard said. "Hundreds of Iroquois armed with Dutch guns attacked the defenseless Huron, burning their villages and carrying away prisoners. Thousands died. Fortunately we managed to lead several hundred Huron families to safety on an island a mile from shore. And from there the following spring you brought them here to Québec."

"While you stayed on and helped the neighboring Algonquin nations defend themselves against the Iroquois. And later, after you returned to Québec, you promised to furnish them with guns. Are you still supplying them with guns?" Father Ragueneau asked.

"Yes I am."

"Even though you know how we feel about this trade?"

"I know your views but I don't share them. In my opinion we must support our allies in whatever way we can."

"Yes," Father Ragueneau said, "we must certainly do that. But with French troops, not by giving them guns. Now that there is peace between France and Spain and the nobles have ended their revolt against the monarchy, the King must send us his best soldiers so we can teach the Iroquois to respect French strength, while at the same time show our allies they can depend on us. It is the only way to impose a binding peace on the Iroquois. When that happens all the nations of this land will fall under our Christian dominion."

"Those are fine words Father but in the meantime the Iroquois are decimating the Algonquin nations with guns they get from the Dutch who trade them for furs plundered from us. Our allies need French guns, and they need them now."

"You know, Médard, there are some who think you are using the Algonquin speaking nations to build an army of your own."

"They need my guns to halt the advance of the Iroquois, their mortal enemy and ours as well."

"Well, at least you don't sell them spirits."

"No I don't, and never will. On that you and I are in complete agreement."

"That is good, for it only degrades them. In this respect you set a fine example for all to follow. Now as to how I might help you in the matter at hand, let me think."

Father Ragueneau looked thoughtful for a moment. Then, as an idea came to him, his face brightened.

"Perhaps if two of our Brothers were to accompany you as missionaries to these new nations the Governor would agree. Indeed, now that Monseigneur Laval is in Québec, and eager to see us continue our work among the scattered nations of this land, it would be difficult for him to stop us. Yes, that might do it."

"Well," I said after we left the Jesuits' residence, "I think our voyage is assured. After all the Jesuits will venture to the ends of the earth to further Christianity for the greater glory of God."

"Perhaps," Médard said. "On the other hand you

may be placing too much faith in the assurances of priests. I think you still have much to learn about the intrigues of men – priests as well as governors."

While we waited for the Ottawa to arrive from the west, the Jesuits – confirming Médard's suspicions – revealed the true reason for their support. Having learned of our plan they conceived their own, which was to get to the Bay of the North by way of the Saguenay River. In this way, perhaps hoping to regain the influence they had over the fur trade when they were in charge of the mission at Sainte-Marie among the Huron.

Since the French first began to fish in the Gulf of St. Lawrence a hundred years ago they had been trading with Algonquin nations living near Tadoussac at the mouth of the Saguenay River, and it had long been known that those nations got their furs from others living farther north near a body of water they called the Bay of the North, which Médard was sure – and the Jesuits did not suspect – was actually Hudson Bay.

One day, hoping to discover our intentions, one of the Jesuit Fathers approached me.

"Pierre," he said, "we are going to sponsor a party of men who will try to reach the Bay of the North by going up the Saguenay River. Naturally, we are anxious to have someone of your experience and courage go with us."

Having been forewarned, I saw they wished to

have me on their voyage in order to make Médard abandon his. But, knowing their expedition could not succeed, I refused to even consider it.

"You'll never make it," I said. "The Algonquin here have told me, though the journey up the Saguenay may be easy, they and the Montagnais farther north will hinder you from reaching it because they depend on trade with the northern nations for their livelihood. Thank you for asking but I prefer to go with my brother."

Nevertheless, before we left for Lake Superior, we learned that two Jesuit Fathers with seven Frenchmen and twelve Algonquin had started up the Saguenay.

Chapter Twenty-One
Arrival Of The Ojibway

In August seven canoes belonging to an Algonquin speaking nation from the west known as the Ojibway arrived in Trois Rivières. Their captain was a well-built man called Wahpus.

"We experienced many difficulties getting here," he said. "Because the Iroquois lay in wait for us on the river the Ottawa use we didn't come down it, but crossed some mountains to get to the river east of it that flows into the River of Canada here."

(Although I preferred the name for the river Wahpus used, the French had renamed it the St. Lawrence.)

"We are glad you arrived safely," Médard said. "We will be ready to leave after you have rested and finished your trade."

While we waited for the Ojibway the Governor of Trois Rivières, Pierre Boucher, paid us a visit. He and Médard were old friends who had served together at Sainte-Marie among the Huron. Later, when Boucher became Governor of Trois Rivières he chose Médard to succeed him as captain of the garrison in recognition of his part in the defense of Trois Rivières during the summer before my return.

After briefly reviewing the state of the town's defenses with Médard, Boucher cleared his throat and came to the true purpose of his visit.

"Médard, I have just received a letter from Governor D'Argenson. He begs me to remind you that you are forbidden to leave for the upper lakes unless you agree to take two of his men with you."

"I have already told the Governor what I think of his servants," Médard said. "Moreover, I consider his demands so unreasonable it would be a pardonable offence if we were to leave without them, especially as we would be acting in the best interests of the country."

"Well," Pierre Boucher said with a shrug, "I have conveyed Governor D'Argenson's instructions and done my duty as you will no doubt do yours."

"We will do what we must," Médard said, adding, "I only hope you won't be blamed for our actions."

Having finished their business, the Ojibway prepared to leave. Before going we gave them gifts of knives, axes and other tools that would make their lives easier.

Speaking for his countrymen, Wahpus said, "We love you like our brothers and wish with all our hearts that you can join us when we leave."

"The Governor forbids us to go unless we take two of his servants with us, which we refuse to do. So wait for us up the river. We will meet you there soon," Médard said.

"We don't know these men and don't want their company, but we will wait two days for you by the side of the lake half a day's journey from here. We want you to come, but if you don't we will go without you."

It was early in the morning when the Ojibway departed. They were not gone long before we thought we better not make them wait, and decided to leave under cover of darkness that same night.

Just after midnight we were ready.

"Be careful, Pierre," Marguérite said, "and watch over my husband. I should die if anything were to happen to either of you."

"Don't worry, we'll be fine and come back rich." Then I left our house and stepped out into the cool night air.

By the entrance Marguérite held Médard close before finally letting him go. From the doorway she watched us head for the village gates. In a low voice choked with tears she called after us, "Be careful my dear brother and my dear husband. Don't forget those who love you."

As captain of the garrison, Médard had the keys to the gates of the fort. We let ourselves out and loaded our belongings into one of the long Algonquin-made canoes we kept by the water's edge.

We embarked and then, having come opposite

the watchtower, a sentry challenged us. "Who goes there," he said

"It is I, Médard Chouart, Sieur des Groseilliers, with my brother, Pierre Esprit Radisson. We are leaving to find the nations that live by the upper lakes."

Everyone – inhabitants and soldiers alike – knew how well we had served New France, and loved us for it. The sentry answered, "May God grant you a good voyage."

With that we set out on what the natives called the River of Canada, and the French the St. Lawrence, and paddled through the night.

Chapter Twenty-Two
Dangerous River

It was near dawn when we reached Lake St. Pierre where Wahpus and his men were supposed to wait for us. But, even though we searched among the marshes along the edge of the lake, we found no sign of them.

Assuming they had gone ahead Médard said, "If we paddle day and night we might catch them before they reach Montréal. But if we don't we will have to forget about getting to Lake Superior this summer as it would be too dangerous to go beyond Montréal without them."

A few miles farther on we saw several canoes coming our way. In case they were Iroquois, we loaded our guns. Fortunately, they were our Ojibway friends.

"If you hadn't come after three days we would have gone back to learn the reason for your delay," Wahpus said when he came alongside us.

It took two days to reach the mouth of the river named after the Ottawa who had been bringing furs down it ever since the Iroquois destroyed Sainte-Marie among the Huron. It was a big river and the main highway between the upper lakes and the St. Lawrence River.

From its mouth to Lake Huron there were more than sixty portages and beside each, where all who went up it had to carry their equipment around powerful rapids, the Iroquois lay in wait.

We hadn't gone far up it when one of our men spotted smoke from a smoldering fire on the west side.

"Ottawa," Wahpus said after some of his men had examined the outlines their overturned canoes traced along the beach. "They left at sunrise in seven canoes."

The Ottawa and the Ojibway were closely related, and Médard knew them well. "When we lived in Sainte-Marie among the Huron they used to bring us furs they got from the Cree," he said, "and for the past ten years I have been supplying them with guns. They are clever traders and excellent hunters, and more experienced with firearms than the Ojibway. If we can overtake them we will be better able to defend ourselves against the Iroquois."

After paddling all day without rest, when we finally caught up with the Ottawa they were surprised and delighted to see us. They were tall and muscular men who wore their hair pulled up and tied over their heads.

"We are on our way back from Montréal," their captain, whose name was Asabonish, said. "Our lives were in peril all the way there. The Iroquois were everywhere and we only escaped their clutches by staying in our canoes coming down the rapids. They wanted our beaver pelts and now they will be waiting to take our guns."

Our party now had fourteen canoes and nearly sixty men who would travel together as far as Lake Superior. Though everyone felt relieved our troops had doubled, we nevertheless remained vigilant.

The following day we had our first encounter with the enemy, who were waiting for us behind a barricade of rocks and trees overlooking a narrow part of the river.

"As I see it, there are only two options," Médard said to Wahpus and Asabonish after beaching our canoes downriver from where the path around the rapids began. "Either we go through the channel and suffer inevitable casualties or we stay and fight."

The two captains conferred with their men.

"My men prefer to fight," Asabonish said, shortly.

"So do mine," said Wahpus.

"Then fight we shall. But before we attack we need a plan. Can you think of a way to overcome them, Pierre? You know how they think."

Following a moment's reflection I said, "They'll be expecting us to charge their fortifications, which would make us easy targets. I have a better idea."

After gathering the men around me and laying out my plan we picked up our weapons and advanced towards the enemy.

While the Iroquois shot at us in vain, our men carrying only their bows and arrows ran from tree to tree. Using the trees for cover, they removed arrows from their quivers. Then, on a signal from their captains, they stepped into the open and released a volley of arrows which arced over the barricade. Then, while the Iroquois dashed here and there, trying to avoid arrows raining down upon them, our men moved closer.

When the Iroquois realized they could not escape they threw strings of wampum over the barricade in the hope of buying peace. The sight of such wealth dazzled our men, as wampum was rare and valued in their country. While they gathered it up the Iroquois flattered them with soothing words, saying what brave men they were, such clever fighters, and so on.

Dismayed to see our men so easily swayed, and an easy victory slipping away, I urged Asabonish to make them fight. "We have the advantage," I said. "Why don't you kill them?"

"We can't without losing some of our own, and my men are not anxious to die. They prefer the certain gain they already have to risking their lives again," he said.

With nightfall approaching we decided to

continue the assault in the morning. But the next day the Iroquois were gone.

Again we set out, on the lookout for more of the Iroquois who patrolled the river constantly. After paddling throughout the morning without incident, in the afternoon we reached a section of rapids where we had to get out and carry everything over a portage.

One of our men, planning to get a fire going at the other end, ran ahead. Halfway across he met an Iroquois warrior coming the other way. As soon as each saw the other they turned around and raced to warn their companions.

On his way back our man met Médard and some of our men who – when they learned the reason for his haste – dropped everything and ran to where myself and the rest were still unloading the canoes.

"Enemy. Enemy," the men with Médard, frightened and out of breath, said. This single word repeated over and over made everyone afraid.

Seeing their fear, Médard urged me to say something to encourage them. "Because they have seen how brave you are, they will listen to you," he said.

"I will do my best."

"Brothers," I said to the men assembled around me, "because I once lived with them you have often teased me about it and called me Iroquois. But because of it, I know them well enough to assure you they are not invincible.

"Besides, our lives are in as much danger as yours. Because they know us, if we are ever captured we will never escape. Myself because I ran away from their country, and my brother because he brings you guns.

"So, you see we are your best friends and have every reason to help you defeat them. Therefore, dear brothers, be brave and let us go and destroy them."

With that, in unison our men let out several war whoops. Then, picking up our weapons, we ran across the portage in pursuit of the Iroquois. Along the way we found bundles of beaver pelts they had dropped.

"Look," Médard said, "they are as afraid of us as we are of them. Moreover these furs were stolen from your country."

"And how many scalps do you think they also took," I said, to which our men responded with a chorus of angry curses.

"Alright then, let us hurry and catch them before they get away."

We reached the river just as a dozen more were landing. The Iroquois reached for their guns, but before they had a chance to use them we shot at them with our guns and bows and arrows.

Panic stricken, the Iroquois threw themselves into the narrow and violent river. If two of their canoes had not arrived just then to save them, we might have killed them all.

Not knowing the size of their war party we took cover in the woods while the rest of the Iroquois escaped to a fort they had on the other side of the river.

"Hurry, bring the canoes," Asabonish said.

The boats arrived and we embarked in the fast moving current. As we approached the other side the Iroquois fired at us but, protecting ourselves with the bundles of beaver pelts they left behind, we made it across unharmed. Only when we landed were they able to kill one of our men but then, seeing themselves outnumbered, they retreated behind their fortifications.

With nothing to protect us except our beaver skin shields we immediately launched a furious assault. As one, we advanced upon them. Meanwhile, they fired at us incessantly.

Thick clouds of gun smoke hung over the battlefield. The obscurity worked to our advantage by making it difficult for them to see us, while we knew exactly where they were. To hasten their defeat Médard tied a barrel full of gunpowder to the end of a long pole and placed it at the base of their barricade, where he detonated it with a bullet.

Though the explosion made a lot of smoke and noise it wasn't sufficient to make a breach in their stronghold. To finish the job, I took another four pounds of gunpowder and wrapped it tightly inside a roll of birch bark; then after inserting a fuse to give me enough time to throw it, I called our men together to explain what to do after the device exploded.

"As soon as their fort is blown apart go in and cut them to pieces," I said.

Seeing their end at hand, the Iroquois began to sing their death songs. Meanwhile I lit the fuse and threw the missile into their midst, where it exploded with a lot of noise.

The blast killed many of them, while the rest tried to escape.

Having lost their weapons in the explosion and blinded by smoke they ran straight into us. Though the two sides hardly recognized one another in all the smoke and dust covering the battlefield our men brought them down with their hatchets. I shot one, and saw Asabonish hack another to death.

Then a sudden thunderstorm came and saved the Iroquois from a certain end. Lightning struck the earth all around and torrents of rain swept over us. Battle cries turned into shouts of alarm as everyone ran for shelter from the downpour and menacing thunderbolts.

When the storm had passed we found we had lost only two of our men and killed ten of theirs. Seven of ours were wounded, though not seriously. The rest of the Iroquois escaped during the tempest.

Though we had great need of it, we slept little that night, staying up to celebrate our victory until dawn.

Médard and I watched with amusement as the Ottawa and the Ojibway danced around a roaring fire surrounded by ten poles planted in the ground, each with an Iroquois scalp tied to its end.

"Why don't you join us," Asabonish said coming over to where we stood.

"It's not our way," Médard said.

"Neither is it ours. But the Iroquois have been so vicious and are so feared this is to show our people they can be beaten. When we find our wives we will celebrate again. Though the Iroquois may be taller and stronger than most men, with guns we are their equal, and when we have more we will keep on killing them until they let us live in peace."

Following our victory we had one more encounter with the Iroquois. But as they outnumbered us, we didn't confront them, managing to get around their ambush under the cover of darkness.

Having barely escaped with our lives we paddled three days without stopping, hardly eating anything except for a bit of salt pork. On the third day we were finally forced to rest. After that we continued up the river without further incident.

Chapter Twenty-Three
God's Country

Sure the Iroquois no longer posed a threat, we paddled at a more leisurely pace, even taking time to enjoy the scenery. At a waterfall along the way some of our men dared me to go under it.

Reluctantly I followed them behind a forty foot curtain of cascading water."Look," one of them said, "how our fearless Iroquois fighter is afraid of a little water." The others laughed and though I laughed with them I must admit to being relieved when we came out the other end.

We continued on our way, making another six difficult portages immediately after the falls. Once we got past the last one the river became narrow and deep.

About two hundred miles up the Ottawa River we turned west onto a smaller one that was often so shallow we had to get out and pull the canoes.

It took two days to reach the end and the watershed beyond which all waterways flowed into Lake Huron. After a short portage, we came to the shore of a shallow and weedy lake.

When Champlain passed this way fifty years earlier it was home to a nation called the Nippissing. But the Nippissing were no longer there, having also gone west to escape the long reach of the Iroquois. Now, except for fish swimming its waters and animals living along its wooded shores, it was uninhabited.

After setting up camp we split up into small groups to search for dinner, soon returning with plenty of meat and fish. After filling our stomachs and a good rest, we paddled across Lake Nippissing to the entrance of the river the French used to go down to get to Sainte-Marie among the Huron.

All along its steep and rocky banks tall pines clung precariously. The current was strong, and in many places huge boulders squeezed the river into dangerous chutes. Going down them, I was amazed at the way our men maneuvered their canoes with so much skill and so little fear.

It took a day to get to the mouth of the French River and the eastern shore of Lake Huron. Then, following the shoreline, we paddled north among countless low islands of pink rock where nothing grew except for a few small pines bent over from strong west winds blowing across the lake. I marveled how clear the water was. Even where it was more than thirty feet deep we could still see bottom.

For four days we followed this treacherous coast, suffering from hunger because there was scarcely any game along its empty shores. The only sustenance we got was from blueberries that grew everywhere, although their season was almost over.

Approaching the north end of Lake Huron I

noticed a range of mountains rising above the horizon. From a distance they seemed snow-capped. I asked Médard about them.

"What from here looks like snow is actually the sun's reflection on the brilliant white rock they are made of. At their base there's a long channel going all the way to Lake Superior. When we get to it we will be sheltered from the hazards of the lake," he said.

But as we approached the entrance to this protected strait the lake rose to dangerous heights. Huge rollers lifted us to their crests from where, after poising momentarily, we surfed down the other side. It got worse. Pink granite cliffs guarding the narrow entrance forced waves at us from all directions. More than once before finally slipping into a quiet waterway, I thought we would be ship-wrecked.

We made camp on the east side of this channel, which was as straight as a Dutch canal and half a mile long. It was full of fish and after making a supper from our catch we smoked our pipes and watched the setting sun turn the white mountain tops just beyond the channel orange. After all the tumult we had been through to get here it felt as though we had arrived in a tranquil paradise.

"Wahpus, what do you call this place," I said.

"Shebahonaning," he said. It meant, "safe canoe passage."

"This is the beginning of our country. From here to the upper lake, the way is sheltered. Safe from both wind and Iroquois. Along the way there are plenty of fish, though not as many as at the entrance to the upper lake."

The following day, after replenishing our supplies with several fat bear and a large number of fish, we paddled out of this channel and across a small bay to an inlet on the other side that was hidden from view.

Cliffs, a hundred feet high in some places, and made of the same white glassy stone as the nearby mountains, ringed the cove. On the west side near the entrance a corner jutted into the water. As we drew closer – with Wahpus guiding us to the right position – I saw a spectacle the likes of which I had never seen before and haven't since.

From a certain distance and from the proper angle it resembled the profile of a man. And with its long aquiline nose, prominent chin, and high cheekbones, this figure – nearly thirty feet high – could have been one of Wahpus's own relatives.

Moreover this engraving of a great warrior – which is how he appeared to me – seemed to burst into laughter as we came nearer. The sun setting behind him threw his stony profile into sharp relief, while shafts of light scattered in all directions from his upturned mouth.

"We are fortunate today," Wahpus said. "When

the chief laughs it is a good sign; it means he is happy and those who see him this way are sure to have good luck. While those who see him frown are sure to encounter misfortune soon after. But, being good-natured, the old chief is seldom sad." With this cheerful comment Wahpus let out his own hearty laugh.

The next day we carried the canoes across a portage at the end of this covered cove to the bottom of a large bay with one of the mountain ranges we had seen from far away on its north side.

Following the north shore to the end of it we paddled across a narrow channel between two bays. Continuing west, we approached a hill of white rock, the size of a small mountain and sparsely covered with pine trees.

"When I was a young man," Wahpus said, "I climbed to the top and stayed several days without eating, waiting for the vision that would reveal my destiny. It came in the form of a rabbit who told me I would be a great warrior, which is how I got my adult name and became a captain in war. All our young men do the same."

On the other side of the channel, across from this rock where Ojibway boys went to dream, three boulders resembling large bells lay stranded on the beach. We stopped to examine them.

"When these rocks are struck," Wahpus said, "the sound they make carries far. When we lived here, whenever strangers – friends or enemies – came this way our lookouts used them to send the news to all the surrounding villages."

All along the way we saw the remains of villages left behind when the Ojibway had to flee ferocious Iroquois attacks.

"Someday we will return to this land of our forefathers," Wahpus said. "And when we do we will be back to stay." To this, his men voiced their agreement.

The next day we continued west on a long and wide channel, staying close to the north shore where the white mountain range continued. Miles away a large island with a high forested back formed the south side of the strait. It was so long we stayed abreast of it for three days.

"Before the Iroquois drove my people away, this island belonged to the Ottawa," Asabonish said when I asked him about it. "There we lived in peace and harmony with our Manitou, the creator of everything. Our corn flourished in its good soil, and in its many bays we caught all the fish we could eat, so we never went hungry.

"Now we are scattered everywhere and sometimes don't have enough to eat. But as soon as we have enough guns to defend ourselves, we will come back to this island where our Great Spirit, Manitou, will watch over us again." Like Wahpus and his Ojibway countrymen, Asabonish and his

Ottawa compatriots – also homesick for their homeland – repeated his pledge. "We shall return," they said in unison.

After losing sight of the big island to the south that had been the home of the Ottawa and principal residence of their Manitou, we finally came to the rapids between Lake Huron and Lake Superior. After making camp at the bottom Asabonish reminisced about the significance of this place before the wars with the Iroquois began.

"In former times," he said, "our people used to gather here in this season to feast on whitefish from the river and geese that came to feed on a grain that grows in surrounding bays. Our relatives came from all around the upper lakes, and here we also traded our corn and wampum with the Cree for their furs."

It certainly was a terrestrial paradise. Besides schools of whitefish swimming at the bottom of the rapids we saw numerous moose and bear. For our suppers we reaped some of its bounty, and gorged ourselves on enormous helpings of fish and meat. After the extreme exertions and long fasts we had endured to get here, being able to eat and rest whenever we wished was heavenly.

But autumn had progressed too far for us to linger. Sadly we prepared to leave, though not before paying homage to the land that fed us so well.

Médard and I watched while the Ojibway and the Ottawa made tobacco offerings on a fire they made for that purpose. One by one they came forward to throw tobacco on it and to express their gratitude. Some thanked the woods for providing us with meat, others the river for giving us fish, the earth for its fruit, and even the rocks in the river for making the fish there easy to catch.

When their ceremonies were over we carried our canoes to the top of the rapids and put them down beside Lake Superior.

Chapter Twenty-Four
Lake Superior

After crossing to the south side of Lake Superior we paddled west, following the coast.

From our canoe Médard called to Asabonish, "I haven't been on this lake before. How far is it to the end?"

"We'll be there before twenty sunrises have past."

"Three weeks," Médard said. "About four hundred miles if we average twenty a day."

The first night, after supper, I watched Médard work on his maps. Carefully, using a piece of charcoal and a roll of birch bark parchment he carried, he drew a line representing the shoreline from where we started out in the morning.

"How do you know where we are," I said, this being the first time I saw him do it.

"Throughout the day I use my compass to take bearings along the course of our journey. That is, how many degrees compared to magnetic north we are heading. I use the latest reading for the direction of the line from the end of the last one. By taking frequent bearings I can chart our course fairly accurately. The distances between each position I guess at based on our usual rate of progress combined with wind and sea conditions."

"And from these measurements you are able to make maps like those both the Governor and Father Ragueneau admired?" I asked.

"Well yes, after correcting my observations for true north. As you will see, on nights when the sky is clear I compare magnetic north by the compass with the north star, making note of the difference and date in a logbook I keep.

"Another thing I do – as well as recording our positions – is make notes of features of interest along the way, which I later add to my maps. Cartography, at which I am only an amateur, is something of an art as well as a science. I've been doing it a long time and enjoy it. Explorers appreciate good maps."

Later, Médard would use these rough sketches to extend the detailed maps he kept in Trois Rivières that then went as far as the rapids between Lake Huron and Lake Superior.

Although we were in a hurry to reach the end of the lake our guides took time to point out the attractions we passed along the way.

One day we stopped at a river where copper nuggets lay on the bottom, and on another at some steep cliffs where Asabonish and Wahpus made tobacco offerings. "What is the reason for doing it here?" I asked Asabonish.

"They are meant to appease the evil spirits living

in these rocks who, when they are angry, can turn the lake wild and cause our canoes to smash against them," he said.

But of all the sights we witnessed the one I will never forget was the enormous sand dunes we stopped at, and that one of our men climbed. They were so high that when he reached the top he seemed no bigger than a crow.

"This is a dangerous place to be in a storm," Asabonish said. "The sand can get whipped up so much it can choke anyone trying to find shelter here. And a really bad one can move these hills from one end of the beach to the other." Fortunately, the day we passed by the weather was fine.

After three weeks we approached the end of the lake, where a long peninsula blocked the way. After a difficult portage to the other side the Ottawa left us and continued overland to search for the rest of their people.

"At the end of next summer we will wait for you at the rapids where the two upper lakes meet," Asabonish said before going.

A few days later we finally reached the southwest end of the lake, where Wahpus and his men went ahead to look for their wives. "When we find them we will return to get your things," he said before they departed.

After the Ojibway left we took advantage of their absence to hide the merchandise we needed to trade with the Cree, planning to retrieve it in the spring.

A week later the Ojibway returned with their wives who carried the rest of our baggage to their village, which was a four day walk west. Until the following spring, when we would set out to meet the Cree, we would be guests of the more than one hundred families living there.

After the first snowfall – because there was not enough game in any one location to feed the entire village – we broke up into smaller bands.

The group Médard and I were with numbered about sixty, and for a while we lived well. In the space of a month we killed enough bear, moose, elk, and deer to last a year. Unfortunately, we saved nothing for the future except skins to make clothing with.

Then it began to snow incessantly and the air got so cold it froze into an icy mist that stuck to trees. Branches snapped and cracked from the cold and weight of snow, which bent them to the ground. Throughout this time, the sky was so dark from constant snow and fog it seemed as though the sun had been eclipsed.

Moreover the snow falling then was so light that – even with snowshoes – it could no longer support our weight which made it impossible to hunt. With nothing set aside from the bountiful days, famine began to stalk every dwelling.

Daily, it got worse. Everyone cried out from hunger. Mothers no longer had milk for their babies, who cried in vain until finally falling silent. When morning came we hardly had enough strength to bury the dead in the snow, while relatives stood by sobbing pitifully.

The first week we ate our dogs. After that we retraced our steps in search of the discarded carcasses of animals we had killed during times of plenty. Next we ate the skins that were to have been used to make our shoes and clothing.

Then, finally, when our bodies could hold out no longer, God's wrath began to be appeased.

A storm from the south brought a warm wind and rain. The thaw, which lasted three days, caused the snow to melt and pack down. When the cold returned the surface had turned to ice which made it possible to walk on without snowshoes.

But what was good for us was not so favorable to deer. With every step they took their hooves punctured the layer of crust covering several feet of loose snow below. Their slow progress made it easy for us to catch them, and cut their throats.

Before long, we began to feel better.

Yet, even these bleakest of times had their lighter moments. One day some of our comrades complained to me that one of our devils must secretly be bringing Médard food.

"Although the rest of us are gaunt from lack of food," one of them said, "your brother's appearance has not changed since our hunger began."

I, knowing it was his thick black beard that made his appearance seem unaltered, said, "If you saw him without his clothes you would soon change your minds."

"Nevertheless," the same man said, "you must like us more than he does since you are as thin as we are." This encounter showed me once again how suspicious natives were of bearded men.

Chapter Twenty-Five
The Sioux

With the famine over and spring in the air, the Ojibway emerged from their winter hunting grounds, and began congregating in a large open area near a clear stream and a grassy meadow where scores of deer grazed.

Before long there were more than five hundred people in the settlement, which we enclosed within a wall of sharpened stakes.

This was also the season when the Ojibway and their neighbors came together to celebrate the end of winter. There were festivals with games and dancing, where friendships were renewed and young men found wives.

A delegation of the Sioux came to take part in the festivities and to become acquainted with Médard and me, the first white men to meet them. The Sioux were renowned for the courage they showed when hunting the enormous herds of buffalo that roamed the vast grassy plains west of us.

Though the Sioux had confederates living in all parts of the land south and west of us, the ones who came to see us used to live in the woodlands around Lake Superior where the Ojibway, after escaping the Iroquois, were now settled. Nevertheless, these two nations were allies, and the Ojibway welcomed the

Sioux as friends.

The day before, an advance party of young Sioux men came to forewarn us of the arrival of their elders. In a clearing outside the fort we helped them erect frameworks of poles for their dwellings, which they called tepees.

The dignitaries arrived with considerable pomp. Young men, wearing only breechcloths with their bodies covered in grease dyed red and hair tied over their heads, and brandishing bows and arrows, led the way. Wearing eagle-feathered headdresses and buffalo skin robes, dignified Sioux elders walked behind them. The last to come were the women, wearing deerskin skirts and leggings, and burdened like mules.

After unfolding their bundles, the women spread out the skins they used to cover the walls of their tepees; then flung them over the frameworks of poles we had assembled earlier. With buffalo rugs for flooring and a fire pit in the center, they had comfortable accommodations in less than half an hour.

The next morning, after they had rested, we invited the Sioux chiefs to a council in a large domed structure the Ojibway had built for that purpose. Since we didn't understand a word of their language, which had nothing in common with the Algonquin language the Ojibway and Ottawa used, we spoke to them through an interpreter.

After a council fire was lit, and everyone had taken their place around it, one of the Ojibway chiefs rose to deliver a welcome speech. After he had finished and sat down, a Sioux chief got up to speak.

"First," he said, "we have come to pay our respects to the French, who are the masters of all things to do with war and peace." The Sioux seated around the fire greeted this declaration with a loud racket – banging their knives, hatchets, kettles, and whatever else was at hand.

"We are also here," he continued, "to honor our friends and to place ourselves under the protection of the French, whom we invite to come to our village, where they will find the doors to the tepees of our daughters and wives open at any time to receive them." Having said this, the chief paused while his two wives stepped forward and presented us with some beaver skins gathered in their country. After we had accepted our presents, he continued.

"At the same time we have come to affirm our alliance with the Algonquin nations and to warn any nation that would wage war upon you that we are ready to die in your defense."

Finally, the chief gave Médard and me each a buffalo robe, saying, "Dispose of us as you will, for the power to defend us is in your hands, as the surest means of victory is to have your thunders," by which he meant our guns. Having concluded his speech, the chief invited Médard and me to join them for a feast.

When the appointed hour came we picked up our bowls and spoons and went with four young Ojibway men who carried twelve of our guns, which were armed and ready to fire – the muzzles having been filled with gunpowder – though without bullets.

In the Sioux encampment, which was outside the walls of our fort, we entered a large ceremonial tepee decorated on the outside with depictions of warriors armed with spears and cloaked in buffalo robes stalking unsuspecting buffalo, as well as celestial objects – the stars, the sun and the moon. Inside, the Sioux were waiting to receive us.

After showing us to our places around a fire burning in the center, four elders approached bringing us a lighted peace pipe. Next, they lit theirs. The bowls of these pipes, reserved for occasions of war and peace, were made of red clay and were as round as a fist and as long as a hand, while the stems were made from hollow reeds five feet long, and as thick as a thumb. Eagle tail feathers dyed many brilliant colors, spread open like a fan, hung from the bowls, while duck feathers and those of other colorful birds hung from the stems.

Finally, they sprinkled our clothing and our weapons with perfume and threw handfuls of tobacco on the fire. All this they did without uttering a word.

While we stood up to smoke our pipe four lovely young women brought bear rugs for us to sit on. Then the oldest of all the elders, rose to speak. He thanked the sun for making this the happiest day of his life by having let him meet such fearsome men as ourselves whose words, he said, made the earth itself tremble. Then he sang a song and when he finished he came and covered us with his robe. Standing naked before us, he said, "Being the masters over us dead or alive, you may dispose of us according to your pleasure." Having spoken, the old man gave us his pipe to smoke while one of the young women lit it with a hot coal.

After we had smoked, I sang a French song, while the Sioux listened politely. When I was finished, Médard, through our interpreter, addressed the gathering. "Have no fear," he said. "We are your brothers and will watch over your lives as though they were our own."

Then, to demonstrate how we would protect them, we fired the dozen guns we brought with us, filling the tepee with smoke and noise. Before the gun smoke had cleared, we drew our knives and swords and slashed the air, cutting imaginary enemies to pieces. Finally, I threw a handful of gunpowder into the fire, where it exploded with a flash of light and a cloud of black smoke. Throughout this drama our guests looked on in terror, not knowing whether to run or stay. Pleased with our performance, we sat down while the elders wore looks of relief.

Now the banquet began. We were served fresh meat and fish and a dish that was new to us, a kind of rice that grew in shallow water, three or four feet deep. Finding it tasted excellent, I asked one of the elders sitting next to us how it was gathered.

"Two people paddle a canoe," he said, "among the rice, which grows thick in shallow water. While one paddles, the other bends the tops down over the boat and beats them with a stick. This loosens the grains and they fall into the bottom. The rice is dried in the sun before being stored for winter. When it is cooked it swells so much that a handful in the pot is enough to suffice a man."

When the feast was over, two of the young women brought us a peace pipe to smoke. One carried the pipe and the other a burning stick. First they offered the pipe to the elder who sat beside us, and when he was finished he asked them to give it to us. Having also smoked, we got up and returned to our lodgings inside the fort.

The next day we invited the principal Sioux to come to the Ojibway council house to receive their presents. When, with great solemnity, they had taken their places our interpreter welcomed them on our behalf. "These presents are to thank you for your gifts and for inviting us to visit your country," he said.

We then distributed our presents among the honored guests. There were six scrapers, two dozen awls, two dozen needles, a dozen little bells, six ivory combs, and a little vermillion rouge for their wives. To the good old man who was the eldest of the elders we gave an iron hatchet and to each of the others, a sword blade. To the two young women who served us, we gave necklaces, which we hung around their necks, and two bracelets for their arms, telling them that our presents were for all the women in general that they might love us and provide us with food when we came to visit them in their tepees. The Sioux thanked us with many "ho, ho's."

Having spent the final days of our stay with the Ojibway in this agreeable way, it was time to leave for Lake Superior, where we would meet the Cree who lived on the north side in the midst of what we believed to be the largest store of beaver in the world. After thanking our hosts we headed back to the lake.

Chapter Twenty-Six
Finding The Cree

A week after leaving the Ojibway we arrived beside the bay where we had left most of our wares last fall.

To avoid arousing the suspicions of some families there for the summer, we went out after dark and found them by the stream where we buried them, still intact and as good as when we left them, showing no signs of rust or any other sort of damage.

With all our merchandise together, we got ready to find the Cree and the Bay of the North.

The bay we were on was at the southwest end of Lake Superior at the bottom of a peninsula that extended far into the lake. The Cree had promised to wait for us on the other side, which our neighbors said could be reached in a day from the tip of the peninsula. Although we had planned to wait until the ice was gone, when we learned some Ottawa on their way up the peninsula were camped on a point not far from where we were, we decided to join them.

After loading our things onto two toboggans we started across the bay, which was frozen solid. But by late morning the surface had turned to slush, which made pulling our overloaded sleds a painful ordeal.

When I saw the strain becoming too much for Médard I offered to take his toboggan, which was heavier than mine. Continuing on, we sank up to our knees with every step. While the wet snow numbed our legs, from the waist up we were soaked in sweat from exertion and the heat of the sun. The going was so slow that even when we could see smoke rising from a point of land just ahead it seemed we would never get there.

"Perhaps we should leave our things here," I said, "and come back in the morning when the surface will be frozen again and we will have help."

"I would be as happy as you to leave our sleds behind. But if our merchandise were to sink through the ice our hopes of returning from this journey with a fortune in furs would be lost as well."

And so we continued. Then, when we were within a couple of miles of our destination, a sudden sharp pain in my right leg made me cry out in agony.

"What's wrong?" Médard asked.

"It's my leg. I can't put any weight on it without excruciating pain."

After examining it Médard said, "I'll have to leave you here and get help. When I've made you comfortable, I'll go as fast as I can to where the Ottawa are camped."

Then he brought the two sleds together and, after helping me remove my wet clothing, made me lie down on top of one before covering me with several dry blankets.

"Don't worry," he said as he hurried away, "the Ottawa will come for you soon." And, in fact, within two hours they did, and pulled me and our toboggans safely to land.

For the next several days, I was in a lot of pain. Unable to rest, day or night, I thought I would never recover. Meanwhile Médard, having diagnosed the injury as a small shin fracture above the ankle, massaged my leg daily with hot bear grease before binding it from ankle to thigh with bandages and splints so I couldn't move it. Finally, at the end of a week, with the help of Médard's remedies, my leg felt much better.

"Well," he said, "you seem to be on the mend, though I think it may be a while before you can walk very far. Meanwhile I will go to the end of the peninsula with the Ottawa and wait for you there. We'll take everything with us so you won't have anything to carry when you are ready to follow."

A few days later a party of men from a nation we had not met before passed through our camp. They spoke the same language as the Algonquin and lived beside a lake called the Winnipeg, or Stinking Lake. They called themselves the Assiniboine, which signified, "fish eaters," having been given this name because they lived on fish from the Stinking Lake.

After saying they were in a hurry to reach their homes, where important business awaited them, they invited me to accompany them. As my leg seemed to have returned to its former strength, I gladly accepted.

I soon regretted my haste. Travelling lightly, the Assiniboine marched briskly up the peninsula. For two days I managed to keep up but on the third my leg hurt too much to continue. Though they were the ones who invited me to come with them, they now left me behind, saying the urgency of their affairs made it impossible for them to wait. Fortunately, before going they gave me a small supply of meat.

Although I didn't know the way, there was nothing for me to do but carry on as best I could. With the sun my only guide, I proceeded slowly and painfully northwards, hoping as I went to find tracks in the snow that still remained on the ground in some places. But I found no sign of human passing.

Alone, I made my way up the peninsula. As evening approached I would search for shelter and gather wood to protect me from the cold night air. After a fire was going I melted some snow to wash down a meager portion of the venison the Assiniboine left me. With my hunger only slightly eased, I slept close to the fire. Mornings, when I woke with my leg stiff and sore, were the most difficult. However, after I started out again the heat of the strong spring sun brought some relief to my pains.

At last, five days after the Assiniboine left me, I heard what sounded like a wolf calling. Listening closely I perceived it was a man and soon after I had answered him the same way he emerged from the bush.

"Greetings brother," he said. "You must be the Frenchman we are looking for, are you not?"

After acknowledging I was indeed the one, he said, "My comrades and I have been searching for you everywhere."

Then we sat down on the ground together, whereupon the man poked around in my bag to see if I had anything to eat. Finding my last piece of meat, about the size of a fist, he began to chew on it without offering me any. I wasn't concerned though, knowing this was nothing other than the etiquette of the land, where a man is expected to share whatever he has no matter how rich or poor he might be.

When his appetite was satisfied he said, "Are you hungry?"

"No," I said although the noises my stomach made testified to the contrary. I spoke this way to show I was as resolute and brave as him.

With a grin the man lit his pipe and opened a deerhide bag from which he took out more than twenty pounds of freshly roasted moose meat wrapped in grease. "Eat," he said.

And I ate, no longer pretending not to have an appetite. After I had eaten as much as I wanted, he offered me his pipe.

"Have courage, brother," he said. "Our camp isn't far from here. Do you know the way?"

"Of course," I said, not wanting to admit I was lost. Nevertheless, he led me to the encampment where I found Médard in the company of some Cree who had come across the lake to look for us.

"The Assiniboine passed here yesterday," he said, "and told us of your plight. We sent volunteers to look for you right away. The Assiniboine said they were in too much of a hurry to help, and only stopped long enough to eat before crossing the lake in canoes."

We sat down then to plan the next leg of our journey. We still had to cross to the other side of Lake Superior before going with the Cree to the Bay of the North. But not wishing to make the Ottawa with us jealous for trading with the Cree without them we told them we were going to do some hunting on the north shore. At the same time we advised the Cree to go ahead, telling them we would find them the next night.

Later, when I told Médard I felt badly for deceiving the Ottawa, he said, "You shouldn't. They wouldn't understand our reasons for going to so much trouble to find a bay we've never seen when there's all the beaver we need right here. Even if I'm right that we can get there in ships it will do no harm to their trade."

The next day before dawn we set out across Lake Superior, and were soon sorry we let the Cree leave without us. Across forty miles of open water we dodged blocks of ice as big as ox carts, coming close several times to being rammed.

By the time we reached the other side it was already dark. Exhausted, and seeing no sign of life, we slept where we landed.

In the morning after paddling out of the small bay we were in and rounding a point on the east side we saw smoke and tents along the shore, not far away.

Chapter Twenty-Seven
Bay Of The North

We stayed a week beside Lake Superior with the twenty Cree families who were living there in domed tents covered with skins. During this time we learned how they lived.

They told us they spent summers on the Bay of the North where they stalked large herds of caribou. In winter, when larger animals were scarce, they lived on rabbits they caught in snares.

In every season they trapped beaver, which were everywhere. But, to be sure there would always be enough pelts to make winter coats with and enough meat for their stews, they never took the young. The men boasted they were the best hunters in the world, a claim we did not doubt as they inhabited the harshest climate of any nation we met.

One day, Médard examined some of the beaver coats that kept the Cree warm in winter. "They are made with the best pelts I have ever seen," he said.

"What makes them so good?" I asked, knowing less about the commercial side of the fur trade than Médard.

"Over the winter a beaver's fur grows thick and the farther north one goes the more luxuriant it becomes. The color is different too. In southern parts it is more of a light brown . . . "

"When I was with the Mohawk the pelts we got from the Erie were like that, and the Dutch told us they were less valuable because of it," I said.

"They were right. Here the beaver the Cree trap have dark brown fur, sometimes almost black. Moreover the pelts they use to make winter coats with are what we call 'castor gras d'hiver,' which is the very best grade. They get them in the fall when they are prime. You know how their coats are made, don't you?"

"Yes, they make them by sewing several skins together with moose sinew. In winter they wear them inside out, and in the spring they discard them. But what makes their old coats so valuable to us?"

"After being worn against their bodies all winter the inside becomes greasy and supple which causes the long guard hairs to fall out. By the time spring arrives there's nothing left except the silky under hair. In this condition they are no longer useful to the Cree. But the downy guard hair that is left is much in demand in Europe, where it is used to make felt hats," Médard said.

"I wonder what the Cree would think if they knew their old coats were used to make hats for the gentlemen of Europe," I said.

"Let's find out. On our next voyage to the Bay we'll bring samples," Médard said. "But concerning our project. I haven't seen furs like these since the

Huron brought them to us at Sainte-Marie among the Huron. They got them from the Ottawa, who got them from the Cree living around Lake Superior. Now you and I are about to discover how to get them at their source."

More than ever now, we were anxious to see the rest of the land the Cree inhabited which held out the promise of such riches. For this reason we hurried to see the clan chieftain.

We found him sitting outside his tent. After explaining the purpose of our visit, Médard picked up a stick and in the dirt made a representation of Lake Superior and another of the Bay of the North, drawing wavy lines on each with an empty space to indicate the land between them.

Then pointing to our location on Lake Superior, he asked, "Is it possible to get to the Bay of the North from here?"

Their chief, a slender and dignified man who wore his long black hair loose and unadorned, studied Médard's drawings. After some thought, he picked up a stick of his own.

"From here," he said, tracing a line on the ground along the north side of Lake Superior, "we have to follow the shore in the direction of the rising sun until we come to the mouth of a river, here, which we must go up to reach the lake where a nation called the Nipigon live.

"At the height of this lake there is another river and at the end of that one we will have to unload the canoes and carry everything across a height of land. On the other side we'll set out on a river that flows towards the Bay of the North." While he talked, the chief traced the course of our journey in the dirt.

"This river flows into yet another, much larger one, that will finally take us to the side of the bitter sea you seek."

"And how long will it take to reach this sea?" I asked.

While waiting for the chief's response Médard and I barely breathed. "It is possible," he said, at last, "to get there in the time it takes the moon to be full twice."

This was exciting news as it meant we could reach the Bay in a month and still have enough time to get back to New France before summer's end. Having determined there was sufficient time to get there, we asked the chief to get his people ready to leave for the Bay of the North.

Early the next morning we piled all our belongings into canoes and set out towards the east. With the wind at our backs we made good time, arriving five days later at the mouth of the river that flowed out of Lake Nipigon.

With darkness approaching the women hurried

to put up tents, prepare beds, and start fires for the evening. While they labored we men smoked our pipes and talked about the journey ahead. Then, after supper and another smoke, everyone retired to their beds to be rested the next morning when we would be on the move again before sunrise.

As our journey continued I got to know the chief's daughter. She was eighteen years of age and pretty. Her name was Amik which in their language meant Little Beaver. Soon we were constant companions.

The third day after passing through a labyrinth of islands we reached the end of Lake Nipigon. Here we entered the river the chief said came from the height of the divide separating rivers flowing into Lake Superior from those going to the Bay of the North.

When it became too shallow to paddle, we attached lines and pulled the canoes with our baggage still in them. Eventually the stream became a brook and we could drag them no farther.

Then began the most arduous part of the long journey to the Bay of the North. Everything had to be unloaded and carried across the watershed. While the men had only birch bark canoes and weapons to carry, the women took the heavier loads.

For hours we climbed through mostly spruce and birch forests, following a trickle of water until it finally disappeared and the ground became firm and dry. Carrying only my gun, I walked beside Amik, bent over under her pack.

I felt sorry for her. "Let me help," I said. But she refused.

"It is a woman's duty to carry the heaviest burdens without complaint, just as a man must hunt and protect his wife and children. It is the wisdom of the Great Spirit that it be so," Amik said.

At the summit of the watershed we stopped. "We'll make camp here," Amik's father said.

After supper, I climbed to the top of a nearby bluff with Amik where we had a clear view of the land all around. Before us the forest spread like a green carpet all the way to the blue horizon. The air was warm and spring fresh.

Sitting on a ledge we waited for sunset. As the sun made its slow descent to the dark forest floor everything grew quiet. In all directions we saw trees and waterways extending across a limitless land. The earth was bathed in a golden light and Amik's dark complexion shone like copper.

"Here, where the waters separate," she said, "is a sacred place."

"Why is that?" I asked.

"You've noticed how everything is still and quiet here, haven't you?"

"Yes, even the sun seems to linger longer than usual."

"In this place the Great Spirit alone reigns, and no evil ones can enter his domain. That is why it's so peaceful and safe."

"Amik, tell me a little about the country we are about to enter."

"Behind us all the lakes and rivers empty into the big lake we came from, but where we are going there are just as many lakes and rivers that carry their water to the Bay of the North. The land is flat and easy to cross and there are many animals and birds, and the rivers and lakes are inhabited by many species of fish that are good to eat. Winters are cold and long, and summers short and hot. Here our people live everywhere. I am sure you will like it."

"I'm happy anywhere you are," I said, putting an arm around her. When she snuggled against me I kissed her.

We kissed some more until she stopped and moved her lips to my ear. "I am yours," she said.

Later, as we lay together admiring the stars, I said, "You were right, Amik. For us, this will always be a sacred place."

The next morning we descended the watershed and by mid-day embarked in our canoes again to start down the river the Cree called the Ogoki. Swollen with spring runoff, the Ogoki carried us swiftly northeast past gray precipices.

The Cree maneuvered their canoes with such skill around granite rocks that could have dashed them to pieces we never lost a single one or any of our precious cargo. Nevertheless, having descended many turbulent rivers before, Médard and I kept up with the rest.

Before they began taking it for granted many of our companions complimented us on our skill with a paddle. "You are almost as good as we are," Amik's father said to me once when we stopped to check our equipment after descending a particularly dangerous series of rapids.

Along the way, wherever there were small tributaries, we saw beaver in ponds held back by dams made from small trees they cut down with razor sharp teeth. At our approach they slapped the water with paddle-shaped tails to warn their kin.

As we went, we met more inhabitants of Amik's wandering nation who lived scattered across this vast land. Sometimes, at the end of a long day, we would stop in one of their villages to spend the night.

Even though it was the middle of May the nights were chilly and the old men still wore their coats of "castor gras."

In the morning, before leaving we gave them some axes and knives, encouraging them to hunt for more beaver. And at each of these villages Médard made the same speech.

"Two years from now we want you to bring your old winter coats to us. Meet us at the Bay of the North where we will have more hatchets and knives for you as well as other useful items. We'll bring them in big ships with sails. Until then, at summer's end, we invite you to bring your pelts to us at the rapids between the two upper lakes," he said.

Even though we were there without the Governor's permission, when Médard spoke he spoke for all of New France, already seeing himself a Seigneur and future Governor. His speeches were inspiring and moved the enthusiastic Cree to swear they would keep their appointments.

After a few days we left the Ogoki and entered a calmer and broader river.

"We are halfway to our destination now," Amik's father said as we started down it.

"And only ten days since leaving Lake Superior," Médard said.

As we descended this new river, that would bring us to the Bay of our dreams, the land slowly changed. The rocky hills that dominated the landscape before gave way to a flat expanse of muskeg and stunted trees. The river grew wide and slow.

"We are coming to the place I told you about the night we first made love at the height of land," Amik said.

Soon signs of the earthly paradise where Amik said I would be happy began to appear. Moose as big as horses come to feed upon tender shoots growing alongside the river watched us go by. Bears in bushes hidden behind high sandy banks stood up to have a better look. One afternoon a wolf ran along a bank of the river, following our canoes.

At night we camped on high ground by the side of the river and fell asleep listening to loons calling and thousands of frogs chirping. Later in the night, wolves howled. And in the morning we woke up to the songs of many species of birds.

And for our breakfasts we dined on fat walleye caught in the river.

Carried forward on the current and our steady paddling we progressed down the river quickly. Rising before dawn we covered more than forty miles a day.

It was still May when we saw the first signs of the Bay. The water began to taste salty and the river rose and fell with the tides. The air was filled with thousands of water birds come to feed in fertile marshes at the river's mouth.

Before finally emerging onto the Bay the river grew wider with several large intersecting islands. At the mouth – where it was shallow – we paddled away from shore in search of a site for our summer homes.

"Keep an eye out for a suitable anchorage for our ships," Médard said as we followed the coast.

South of the one we came down, the Cree erected their dwellings at the mouth of another large river. When they were finished they celebrated the start of summer with feasts and dancing.

There were marriage banquets too, for this was the season when the scattered bands of Cree met to renew old friendships and to take new husbands and wives.

The marriages were simple. The groom gave presents to the bride's parents and if they accepted the couple was married.

I gave Amik's father several axes and knives and some awls to his wife. Then after our marriage, according to their tradition, Amik and I lived as husband and wife in her parents' tent. They called me Son, and I called them Mother and Father.

Summer came to the Bay early that year. The sun grew hot and the Cree shed their winter clothes. Soon everyone turned dark under the hot sun. We fished and hunted every day, as there were many animals around – especially flocks of white geese.

As the summer passed, I grew to admire the Cree more and more. They were a gentle and kind race who, unlike the Iroquois and other nations Médard and I had met, didn't torture their prisoners.

"It's indecent for men to be so cruel," Amik's father said when I asked him about what his daughter had told me.

"She also said you treat animals with respect. When I lived with the Iroquois we often hunted just for sport. Although that might be because they have guns which makes it easier to kill, animals as well as men."

"We only kill what we need. Neither do we waste anything. We use every part. Bones for weapons and tools, skins for clothes, and meat to eat. And to preserve future generations we let the young live."

With lots of leisure on our hands, Médard and I explored the coast up and down as far as the mouth of a river known today as the Rupert.

"This will be an excellent harbor for our ships," Médard said.

Later, back at the village, I asked Médard to go over his plan for returning in ships.

"It would be nice if we had some beer to discuss our business with," I said after we found a quiet place to sit.

"I am sure there will be room on our ships for a barrel or two. But what would you like to know?"

"All right, to begin with, when we come back in ships how will we get here? And when and where will we get the things we need to trade?"

"After studying Henry Hudson's voyage, I have given this matter a great deal of thought," Médard said.

"He's the reason the English call this Hudson Bay."

"They do, and from what I have read and heard he arrived in the middle of summer when the bay was clear but left too late and got caught in the ice."

"How do we avoid the same fate?"

"We'll leave Québec as soon as the ice is gone and sail down the St. Lawrence River; then up the coast of Labrador where there are many coves to find shelter in during a storm. By the time we reach the mouth of Hudson Bay the ice will be gone."

"Will we take the furs to France?"

"No. My idea is to return to Québec in time to meet the last ships to France. The following spring they'll return with our order for more goods and guns, and we'll do it all over again."

"Wouldn't it be easier to take the furs directly to France?"

"Perhaps, but I've made my life here, and there's

more opportunity in this country. Here I will be a Seigneur with land and farms, and when I become Governor I'll build up our defenses against the Iroquois and expand the trade. You, of course, will be my right hand man."

"I like your plan. The way we came is too risky."

"We were lucky to get here without the Iroquois killing us or drowning in the rapids on the way. Besides, canoes can't carry enough supplies or furs. Ships are what we need."

Near the end of June, we got ready to leave. Having seen the country firsthand, we now knew the best way to harvest the furs of this vast and rich country was to come by ship.

After an enjoyable stay, we left the Bay of the North – rather Hudson Bay as Médard's calculations confirmed – reluctantly. Though winter came early to these parts there was still another month of summer left. Taking advantage of the good weather, a number of Cree men came with us, their canoes loaded with pelts from old beaver coats.

The saddest part of leaving was saying farewell to my beloved Amik. But as much as I loved her I had to go, though I promised to come back soon.

With my arm around her waist, which had expanded a little over the summer, she accompanied me to the landing place. Before we embarked I held her in my arms for a long time.

"When you return your son will be able to walk and beginning to talk," Amik said after a final tearful kiss.

"When I come back I'll bring him – or her – new toys and blankets."

"Which I'll trade you for his first winter's beaver coat."

Chapter Twenty-Eight
Montréal Trade Fair

Montréal, New France – 1660

With Asabonish and three hundred of his men, we raced down the Ottawa River in sixty canoes.

"Where are the Cree?" he had asked when we met up with them at the rapids at the entrance to Lake Huron. As arranged last fall, Asabonish had been waiting for us there.

"They were with us up until two days ago," I said. "But on our way down a river to get here from the Bay of the North we saw signs some Iroquois had passed by and even though we could tell from their tracks there weren't many of them, it was enough to terrify the Cree, and they turned back."

"If they had only stayed with you a little longer we could have protected them," Asabonish said. "As you can see I've come with reinforcements."

"And on the return from Montréal they would have had guns," I said.

"Even with guns I don't think they would make the journey. It's too far from home for them and they don't like to fight. In my opinion they will always be content to have us go to them," Asabonish said.

"The worst of it is we couldn't bring all of their furs with us," Médard said.

About forty miles above Montréal, at the rapids known as the Long Sault, we made a grisly discovery. In a charred and burned out fort we found the skeletons of Dollard des Ormeaux and sixteen other Frenchmen, together with those of forty Huron and four Algonquin.

Later we learned what had happened to them. For seven days they fought off an Iroquois war party on its way to attack Montréal until, finally, they ran out of ammunition and were overwhelmed.

The battle took place in May, and when we passed by in the middle of August all that remained to tell the tale of this epic struggle were the bleached bones of Dollard and his brave band of men.

The discovery filled our hearts with renewed dread for that implacable enemy. Afraid they might be waiting for us along the portage we risked our lives and went down the thundering Long Sault rapids in our canoes. After getting soaked and tossed about in mountains of rushing water we emerged intact; nevertheless, too afraid to rest, we paddled through the night.

Early the next morning as we approached Montréal a new worry began to trouble us. What if the Iroquois, emboldened by Dollard's defeat, had gone on to destroy the settlement?

But our concerns vanished when we heard cannons booming from the ramparts and inhabitants waiting for us at the docks firing their guns into the air.

When we landed they greeted us with food and drink, relieved we were safe and happy to see the furs we brought that once again would save the colony from ruin.

As we disembarked Charles Le Moyne, Médard's old friend from Sainte-Marie among the Huron and present-day business partner, stepped out of the crowd.

"Médard, you old rascal," he said. "I knew we could count on you to outwit the Iroquois."

"Charles, my dear friend, I am so relieved to see you alive. After our discovery at the Long Sault I never thought to see you or anyone else here again."

After they had embraced, Le Moyne said, "I almost went with them. But because it was seeding time I stayed behind. After all, what good would it have been to save the inhabitants' lives if they were left with nothing to eat. So, you see, if duty hadn't kept me here you might have come across my poor bones too.

"But enough of this gloomy talk. We have business to discuss. Here you are with the finest lot of furs I've seen in years while my warehouse is chock full of merchandise I'm sure your men will find of great interest."

"I'm sure they will. And their guns? Do you

have them?"

"Of course, my friend. And as always, we'll take the furs to pay for them to the King's Stores and I'll give you your share of the profits."

"This arrangement has served us both well, and when I tell you what I have planned for the future you will see that our prospects look even brighter."

"Well, then, this calls for a celebration. After we've been to the King's Stores come with me to my establishment on St. Paul street where we can discuss our mutual interests in comfort."

"Nothing would please me more, old friend. After the ordeals and deprivations we have experienced, some of your wine and cheese will be most welcome."

Before leaving with Le Moyne, Médard took me and Asabonish aside.

To me, he said, "Make sure our Ottawa friends are treated well."

To Asabonish, "When I return from my meeting I will have guns for you and all your men. As we agreed I am taking enough of your pelts with me to pay for them. My brother will help you set a price for the rest."

After Médard and Charles Le Moyne were gone Asabonish summoned the other captains, and we all met beside the river. At the same time, behind us the merchants of Montréal began assembling their wares on the grounds outside the gates.

While waiting for trading to begin, the merchants persuaded their wives to bring bread and cheese and some of the kettles of stew and soup always simmering on the hearth.

"We are going to be rich," I heard more than one tell his wife. For many who had gone into debt to acquire merchandise for the trade it was their last chance. The Iroquois blockade over the past two years had brought the fur trade to a standstill and, naturally, after such misfortunes the merchants wanted to make the most of the occasion.

Their wives, too, readily set aside their customary worries and allowed themselves to share their husbands' optimism. Wearied by the harshness of life in Canada and the constant Iroquois attacks, everyone was anxious to seize upon the first piece of good fortune to come their way in a long time.

With this in mind they hurried to fill their baskets with the most appetizing things they could find. Being harvest time their pantries were well stocked with preserved fruit, cheeses and bread, and with their children's help they soon returned with steaming kettles and baskets full of food. While the Ottawa and I went over the value of their furs the square behind us began to take on the character of a fair.

The twenty captains of the three hundred

Ottawa men gathered around as I laid a pelt of the finest grade of "castor gras" on the ground.

"A pelt such as this one is worth this many knives like these," I said placing six long knives next to it. "Or eight of these," I said replacing the six long knives with eight smaller ones. "Or this many hatchets, beads, kettles and tobacco," I said replacing each item in turn with two iron axes, half a pound of beads, a kettle, and a pound of tobacco.

In the same way I showed them a woolen blanket cost five pelts, while mirrors and combs were worth two. Likewise, I showed them the value of fishhooks, needles, and awls.

"Everything the French possess has a value in beaver pelts," I said, "though you can bargain with the settlers to get the best price."

"Well," I said to Asabonish after tutoring his captains as well as I could, "I think your men are ready to trade."

Then, carrying a bundle of pelts each, the captains approached the merchants and began cautiously to inspect their wares, spread out neatly on red blankets. The merchants greeted them with smiles while their wives, in long blue dresses and white bonnets, offered food to the Ottawa, while looking away from their scanty deerhide loincloths.

As the trade proceeded, Jesuit priests in black cassocks wandered through the crowd. With eyes trained to find sin they looked for signs of brandy that would corrupt the Ottawa and make them give away their furs. But they found none, and the trade continued in a peaceful and good-natured fashion.

The Ottawa were experienced traders who, long before the French arrived, had traded furs they obtained from the Cree for Huron corn and wampum. Having once again proved their skill at bargaining, they came away pleased with the merchandise they got in exchange for their furs.

The merchants also seemed satisfied, though some may have wondered if they hadn't sold their wares too cheaply. Nevertheless, they made a profit. Enough to continue in the fur trade, which seemed more appealing than ever.

Now in a mood to celebrate, the inhabitants brought out their musical instruments. The dusty common soon filled with men and women who began to dance the minuet to the accompaniment of guitars, recorders and violas. Everyone gathered around the players, some to watch and some to dance. Attracted by the music, the Ottawa joined in and, with shuffling feet, followed the dancers around in circles. The inhabitants laughed at the spectacle, while the good-natured Ottawa, laughing in return, continued to dance their way.

While the inhabitants and the Ottawa amused themselves, the Jesuits stood by with disapproving looks. They frowned on dancing, and the only music that appealed to their ears was religious hymns and chants. Shaking their heads, they were heard to say the fur trade would corrupt the morals of the inhabitants. But the merrymakers ignored the scowls of the good Fathers and continued with their entertainment.

As darkness approached bonfires were lit. And though the August night was clear and cool, the dancing and a little brandy kept us warm.

"This is good," Asabonish, with whom I shared some, said. "Although there's not enough."

"My brother doesn't want you or your men to drink too much. He thinks it will cloud your judgment and make you give away your furs."

"Your brother has always been good to us and treated us fairly. It's one of the reasons we trust and love him so much. We also remember how he brought us guns and helped us against the Iroquois after they had vanquished the Huron."

Nevertheless, there was just enough brandy to keep everyone cheerful as we danced away the night.

While the Ottawa amused themselves, I sat beside a fire surrounded by a knot of young men and boys from the village who begged me for stories of our adventures. As it gave me great pleasure to relive the events of the past year, I happily obliged.

In vivid detail I described our experiences and the many exotic nations we encountered during our journey. After I told them of the riches to be had in the land around Lake Superior, many thought they should also visit the "upper country." I encouraged them to go, saying there was enough beaver for everyone.

Chapter Twenty-Nine
The Governor's Retribution

Before we left Montréal Médard told me about our latest agreement with Charles Le Moyne.

"As in the past, we agreed to share the profits on guns we sell to the western nations. I told him our new allies, the Cree, needed several hundred," he said.

"But we won't be back this way to deliver them," I said.

"I know, but others will. Le Moyne is backing some men who went with the Ottawa. Our guns are making the rivers safe again. Trade with the Algonquin nations in the west will prosper and Montréal will be its center."

"What about our plans to bring ships to Hudson Bay. Did you tell him about that?"

"No. I told him that although we came close to the Bay of the North we didn't get that far. Pierre, no one must know about our discovery or our plans. In the future, if anyone asks, tell them what I told Charles Le Moyne. No one but you and I can know that the Bay of the North and Hudson Bay are one and the same."

With our business done we prepared to leave. Having been away a year we were anxious to see our family and friends again. We left for Trois

Rivières in five of Le Moyne's river boats equipped with sails and small cannons. With twenty of his men along to protect us and our furs, only one concern disturbed our peace of mind.

What kind of reception would the Governor of New France give us? Though we left without his permission we hoped the valuable cargo we came back with would convince him we had only acted in the King's best interest.

But Monsieur D'Argenson's opinion of us had not changed. Before Médard even had a chance to kiss his wife, our furs were seized and he was locked up. With his friend Pierre Boucher no longer the Governor of Trois Rivières, he was made to cool his heels in jail while the new Governor waited for instructions from Québec.

They came soon enough. We were both to be taken into custody and delivered to Québec.

Which is how a few days later we found ourselves once again inside Château St. Louis. After waiting nearly an hour in a chilly anteroom the same somber looking secretary as on our last visit came to show us to his master's quarters.

Since we last saw him the Governor's appearance had changed for the worse. Where formerly he seemed young and vigorous, he now appeared old and worn. Even his usual fine clothes and powder were not enough to disguise his poor health.

We had heard rumors the disagreements between the Governor and Bishop Laval had grown worse, and that now he was eager to leave the colony that had become such a frustration to him.

Appraising his bitter countenance I worried his difficulties and poor health might make him unsympathetic to our cause. While he glared at us from across his desk we held our peace. Finally, he spoke.

"Gentlemen, I'm afraid you have put me in an awkward position. On the one hand you are without a doubt responsible for saving the colony from bankruptcy. Yet, on the other . . . "

For a while he seemed unable to go on. Then, with face reddening and voice rising, he continued.

"On the other hand you have flagrantly challenged my authority as Governor of New France. You must know that observance of my rule is as absolutely necessary for the prosperity of the colony as obedience to Louis XIV is to the stability of France."

When again the Governor paused blood began to drain away from his face, which resumed its normal sallow color. Then, in a calmer voice, he said, "I have here the receipts for the beaver pelts you brought back from your illegal expedition. The factor of our warehouse at Trois Rivières informs me the value of your furs has been set at 70,000 pounds.

"However, your disobedience of our authority cannot go unpunished. Therefore, for having left Trois Rivières when you had been ordered to remain, we are levying a fine of 4,000 pounds, which will be used to improve the fortifications of the village."

"But Monsieur D'Argenson," Médard said, "as captain of the garrison I could come and go as I pleased."

"That did not give you the right to explore the King's lands without my permission. Nevertheless, I am a reasonable man. So as a sign of our gratitude for your generous donation, you have our permission to display your coat of arms above the entrance to the fortifications of Trois Rivières."

The prospect of having his coat of arms nailed to the walls of Trois Rivières appealed to Médard, whose vanity was as great as the Governor's. Having been granted this small concession, he seemed ready to accept the inevitability of another tax.

But the Governor had saved the worst for last. "In addition, you must pay the King 14,000 pounds, which is the usual tax of one fourth. Furthermore, because you did not have a permit from me and were consequently engaged in the fur trade illegally, you must pay me a fine of 6,000 pounds, which will be used for the improvement of the country."

This time I was the one to protest the injustice of the Governor's punishments. "For the improvement of the country, you say. More than likely the country will never see a penny. Rather, I think you will keep it for the maintenance of your horses and carriages when you return to Paris."

Again the Governor reddened. Though this time I was sure it wasn't from anger but from shame, for there was more than a grain of truth in what I alleged. Nevertheless, the bastard recovered quickly from whatever embarrassment he may have felt.

"I warn you, Monsieur Radisson, you go too far," he said. "Remember, my authority here is absolute. So far I have treated you and your brother-in-law with lenience. Do not force me into harsher action. Besides, are you and your relatives not also inhabitants of this country? And do you not wish to spend your lives here? Think, then, how charity serves us all and be satisfied with what we have left you."

Having robbed us of some 24,000 pounds, the Governor sought to placate us with a little food and wine. But we refused his false hospitality, saying urgent business awaited us in Trois Rivières.

So we left the Governor, who had no friends in New France, to contemplate the splendor our money would afford him in Paris.

Chapter Thirty
Jesuit Dreams

Before leaving Québec, we stopped at the Jesuits' residence to visit Father Ragueneau to whom we had promised to give a full account of our latest adventures and discoveries.

"Welcome back," he said in the foyer where we met. "I've heard about your troubles with the Governor. I hope your meeting with him went well, and you were able to resolve your differences to your mutual satisfaction."

"On the contrary," Médard said."After saving the country, I expected to be rewarded for our services. Instead we were fined and put in jail like common thieves. Such an injustice cannot go unanswered. The Governor has insulted my honor, and I intend to present my case in France to the King, himself."

"My son, I beg you not to do that. You will only waste your time and your money." As Médard made no reply to this wise piece of advice, Father Ragueneau asked us to honor him with a complete account of our recent voyage.

While he listened closely, we recounted the highlights of our journey to the land around Lake Superior. He interrupted often to ask questions, and when we reported our conversations with the Sioux elders who had come to visit us over the winter when we were with the Ojibway and told us of a salty sea beyond a range of snow-capped mountains to the west of them, he became animated.

"It can only mean one thing," he said. "We know that the known parts of North America are surrounded by water, in the south, the east, and even the north, though that way is obstructed by ice. Now, from what you have told us, there can be only one conclusion. And that is that the whole of North America is surrounded by water, and the western sea the Sioux told you about must lead to China. If we can only find a passage through the northwest we will be able to bring back the riches of that fabled land."

Though it was the dream of a northwest passage to China that stirred the imaginations of Father Ragueneau and the merchants of Europe, we had a more modest and, we thought, practical dream. We only wished for ships to take us to Hudson Bay, where a vast wealth of furs were ours for the asking.

But that was a secret we would share with no one, not even a priest.

Chapter Thirty-One
Médard's Profligate Ways

Back in Trois Rivières, it didn't take long for Médard to find a use for the 46,000 pounds the Governor let us keep.

His first purchase was a piece of property on Rue Nôtre Dame within the walls of the fort. It was a double lot with a dilapidated building on it. But it was on the main street, close to the river and ideally suited for our new headquarters.

"We'll tear down this old log cabin," he said as we toured the property, "and erect a three storey stone building in its place. Our offices will be on the ground floor, and there will be a warehouse and living quarters above. Le Moyne will be envious."

Headquarters on Nôtre Dame was only the start of Médard's grand vision.

On Cap de la Madelaine on the property Marguérite's former employer, Jean Godfrey, Sieur de Lintot, gave her on the occasion of her marriage to her late husband, Jean Véron, he built a stone manor with enough room for their six children as well as quarters for the servants and myself. And on the main floor there was a spacious room with polished pine plank floors where Médard and his wife could entertain the leading citizens of Trois Rivières in splendor.

In the fall he joined Jean Godfrey and other

prominent men on hunting excursions.

Yet, all the distractions of a seigneur's life were not enough to satisfy him. Still brooding over the Governor's mistreatment, he announced one morning he would be leaving soon for France.

"I cannot ignore such injustices without seeking redress," he said.

"The King won't listen to you," Marguérite said. "No matter how just your cause the Court simply will not support you against the Governor. Monsieur D'Argenson is one of them. In their eyes we are mere colonists deserving only to be paid with fair words and promises."

Though I took my sister's side, Médard wouldn't listen to our arguments. "Nothing will change my mind. In any case I must go there to find ships for our voyage to the Bay of the North."

Near the end of November, he sailed from Québec on the last ship of the season. Then the St. Lawrence River froze, leaving the inhabitants of New France isolated and cut off from the mother country through another long and cold winter.

Over the six months Médard was away enjoying the pleasures of France, Marguérite and I managed our extensive holdings in Trois Rivières.

I maintained the properties and cared for the oxen and pigs we kept for our own use and to sell to the inhabitants.

Throughout Médard's absence, Marguérite carefully managed the 10,000 pounds he had left in her care. I have often thought since how we might all have been better off if he had entrusted her with all of our profits.

The next spring Médard returned, having failed to persuade the court of Louis XIV to overturn the Governor's fines. Then, soon after his return, the Vicomte d'Argenson having been vindicated by his master left for France too, with his pockets full of our money.

Médard's appeal to the King had cost a great deal. While his petition made the rounds of administrators Médard, who had bought himself a new wardrobe, passed his time in lavish apartments where he entertained the ladies and gentlemen of the Court in style.

Moreover, he came back with new furniture for the estate as well as clothes for Marguérite and the children. A young niece, who gave birth to a child just before their departure, came with him. He also brought back a new servant girl to help in the house.

Although unsuccessful at Court, Médard did find a ship for our maiden voyage to Hudson Bay.

"It's a solid vessel," he said. "And it is to be delivered to Percé next spring."

Through all this prodigality, he managed to spend almost all our capital. Little remained besides the balance of the 10,000 pounds he had left in Marguérite's care. Understandably, she was upset.

"And when that's gone what are we to live on?" she asked one evening while we sat around an imported mahogany dining room table, enjoying a bottle of the wine Médard brought back from France. "There are servants to be paid, fields to plant, and animals to feed. And there's the cost of boarding the boys in Québec while they are at school. With all our obligations, the money we have left won't last more than a year. And then what?"

"Don't worry," Médard said. "Today we are one of the richest families in all of New France. And when Pierre and I return from our next voyage, our wealth then will begin to rival even the greatest fortunes of France."

Throughout the following winter we prepared for our voyage to Hudson Bay. Peas from the summer harvest were dried and stored in canvas sacks to prevent moisture from spoiling them. Boiled to mush and mixed with salt pork, they would be our principal nourishment when we were at sea.

Before we left, Charles Le Moyne sent us everything we needed for our trade with the Cree – knives, axes, kettles, awls, fishhooks, and guns, too.

For ease of handling, we packed everything into

bundles small enough to be carried by one man.

Finally, when the St. Lawrence River was free of ice we prepared to leave for Percé to take delivery of our ship when it arrived from France. Before leaving we engaged a crew of nine men, all in good shape and ready to risk their lives for us. We told them, and everyone else, we had decided to try to reach the Bay of the North by way of the Saguenay River because, we said, it was a shorter route with little to fear from the Iroquois.

After loading everything into five long canoes, we said farewell to Marguérite and the children. They stood by the water's edge, the children by Marguérite's side and little Marie Antoinette – who came into the world while her father was away in France – in her arms.

Though knowing she might never see us again – for our sake – she put on a brave face. We were leaving her with a large family to care for and properties to manage, with not enough money and only a promise to return in the fall.

Before we departed – as if to confirm her worst fears – Médard left Marguérite his power of attorney, so in our absence she might conduct our affairs as she saw fit.

Chapter Thirty-Two
The Betrayal

After paddling two days we passed by Québec in the middle of the night.

The next morning a fast current and an ebbing tide carried us around the north side of Ile d'Orléans, past settlers behind their oxen plowing steep strips of recently cleared land.

Only when we reached Tadoussac – one hundred miles downstream, and the last settlement under the Governor's jurisdiction – did we allow ourselves to rest.

While the men refreshed themselves, Médard composed a letter to the Governor of New France. When he had finished he handed it to me. "Read it and tell me what you think," he said.

After the usual introductory formalities, it said:

"We are sorry to have missed you on our way through Québec. However, since this time we are not planning to cross any of the King's land we didn't think we needed to stop for your permission. By the time you receive this we will be out to sea and on our way to the Bay of the North. On our return this fall we will have a ship's hold filled with prime beaver pelts worth at least 500,000 pounds. Considering the contribution 125,000 could make to the prosperity of New France, I trust you will be more reasonable than your predecessor and be satisfied with the tax of one fourth, which we will gladly pay – but no more."

And ended this way, "I remain, your humble servant, Médard Chouart, Sieur Des Groseilliers."

"Reasonable and respectful," I said. "With this he won't be able to say we left without his knowledge."

We gave the letter to a settler who promised to take it to the Governor on his next visit to Québec. Then we brought the men together and told them about the change of plans.

Claude, a large burly man, acted as their spokesman.

"It's all the same to us," he said. "Might even be a little easier since there will be no portages to carry the baggage over. On a ship we'll be able to carry beer too, won't we?"

"Of course, and since we'll be able to carry more furs there will also be more money for everyone," Médard said.

A week later we approached Percé, famous for a rock at its entrance resembling the hull of a huge ship. After going around it we entered a deep and sheltered harbor where a number of vessels, here to catch some of the millions of cod swimming in the surrounding waters, were anchored.

On a promontory overlooking Percé's rock, the

Jesuits oversaw a small log chapel with a large wooden cross in the ground beside it. As we landed Father André Richard came down to greet us.

After a few pleasantries he said, "Médard, may we have a word in private?"

After they were out of earshot I watched as the conversation became animated and Médard, taller and bigger, began wagging a finger in front of Father Richard's nose. When it came to an abrupt end Médard came striding back. Halfway, he stopped and waited while I walked down the pebbly beach to join him.

"Those scheming bastards," he said when I met him. "Somehow, the Jesuits got wind of our plans and prevented the Protestant merchants of La Rochelle from delivering our ship. Now, having failed to get there without us, they have the nerve to ask us to return to Québec and take them up the Saguenay River to the Bay of the North."

"What did you tell him?"

"I refused, of course. Adding, if you are so damned eager to go there you can find your own way."

"What are we going to do now? Without a ship, we can't get to Hudson Bay from here."

"I have a plan," Médard said. "Acadia isn't far from here, and there we can sell some of our merchandise to my friend Nicholas Denys for a good price. And with the profits we'll engage another ship and go there after all."

"Will we be able to find one in Acadia?"

"Not likely. We will probably have to go to Boston. And after we've been to Hudson Bay perhaps we'll do as the Jesuits fear and take our pelts to the English who couldn't treat us any worse than our own countrymen have."

"In my opinion they would deserve it," I said.

"In future, we'll think more about our own welfare rather than worry about a country that doesn't appreciate us. What do you think, Pierre?"

"You know I will go wherever you take us. Politics aren't important to me. All I want is to see new places and discover new people."

"What would I do without you," Médard said. "You are the only one who understands what I am trying to do. Why should it matter to anyone if we get rich while helping the country? Yet, it seems the lords of both Old and New France – and now the Jesuits as well – want to keep us from benefiting the country as well as ourselves. Well, dear brother, from now on it's going to be us against them."

Before we left Father Richard took me aside. "My son," he said, "I don't think you know what kind of man your brother-in-law is."

"Why do you speak about him this way?"

"Because he wishes to ruin the country. That is why we prevented him from carrying out his plans."

"Why do you accuse us of wanting to harm the country? In the past has it not benefited from our commerce with distant nations?"

"Of course it has, my son. But now your brother-in-law wants to take that trade away from us. If we were to let you go to the Bay of the North by ship, as you planned, you would no longer need to bring your furs to Québec. You could go straight to France, or even to England if you chose. Without the fur trade New France cannot survive, and all our good work here would be lost."

"With respect, Father, my brother and I are loyal subjects. This was not at all our plan. We meant to base ourselves in Trois Rivières, where we have family and property, and an interest in the trade with the Algonquin nations that live around the upper lakes. So, you see Father, your fears are groundless and because of them you have done grievous harm to us and to New France."

"Nevertheless it's not right to destroy a country in such a manner, nor to wrong so many inhabitants. That is why I implore you, Pierre, leave your brother-in-law before it's too late. Go back to Québec, and lead us up the Saguenay River to the Bay of the North."

"I cannot – my fortunes are tied to his. Wherever

he goes, I shall follow," I said.

"As you wish, Pierre. But when, someday, you see we were right, remember it was I who warned you."

We left Percé on a supply ship which took us to St. Pierre in Acadia, where we met Médard's friend Nicholas Denys who had lived at his trading post on Cape Breton Island for thirty years. Today a man of sixty, he had white hair and a long white beard.

After trading much of our merchandise – meant for the Cree – for some of his beaver pelts and moose skins, Denys invited us to dinner.

"Go to New England," he said, as we washed down big moose steaks with some of his good wine. "There you will be well paid for your furs and find men ready to invest in your venture. Here, the nobles of France are too busy battling one another for control of Acadia to be of use. If I could help you, I would. I once had a thriving timber and fur business here, but the squabbles and greed of the nobility have almost ruined it."

"Denys is right," Médard said afterwards. "Let's waste no more time here. We'll go to New England where we will surely do no worse than in New France."

We went to tell the men about our change of plans.

"Men," Médard said, "the Jesuits have betrayed us. Because of their meddling, the ship that was to meet us here couldn't come. If it had we would have gone in it to the Bay of the North and returned to New France with our holds full of beaver pelts. Even so, I think there is still time to get there if we go to New England for another ship. I hope some of you will stay and join us in this great enterprise."

Claude was the first to speak. "I didn't sign up to become a traitor to my country," he said.

"I understand," Médard said. "As for the rest of you, anyone who wants to return to your home can and we will pay you for your trouble."

After talking it over among themselves only three of the nine men who started with us decided to accompany us to New England.

Finally, after a lot of hard work, and danger from troops belonging to French nobles then fighting over Acadia, we arrived in Port Royal where two hundred and fifty Frenchmen lived under the English flag.

A few days later we boarded a ship for Boston. The year was 1662. Only a few years before, the English had taken Port Royal from the French. Now, two of France's most faithful servants, myself, Pierre Esprit Radisson, in the company of my brother-in-law, Médard Chouart, Sieur Des Groseilliers, were going over to the English too.

Under full sail, Médard and I stood on the aft deck watching Port Royal recede into the horizon.

"It's an impressive sight," I said

"Yes, though it's sad to see the Cross of St. George flying over it instead of the Fleur-de-lis. You know, this is where Champlain spent his first winter before he made Québec the capital of New France," Médard said.

"And now Port Royal is in the hands of the English, as we will soon be."

"Yes, but it is not we who desert the French," Médard said. "Rather, it is the rulers of France who have abandoned us. But, for all their power they do not have the strength to keep us from returning to the people and country we love." Then he fell silent. Leaning on the rails and watching the vast land behind us vanish into the distance, he appeared lost in his thoughts.

Having nothing more to say either, I gazed into the ship's wake, thinking about the places I had been and the people I met along the way. Good men, like Father Simon Le Moyne and Father Paul Ragueneau. Brave ones too, like Wahpus and Asabonish. And the gentle women I knew and loved – my sister, Marguérite; my Mohawk mother, Gannendaris; and my lovers, Conharrasan and Gahano; and especially my wife, Amik.

Yet, as much I would miss them and my adopted

country, I could not help but also wonder about what new adventures lay ahead.

THE END

Epilogue

After sailing from Port Royal in 1662, Radisson and Des Groseilliers spent three years in Boston without finding a ship able to take them to Hudson Bay.

Their luck changed in 1665 when they met Colonel George Cartwright, one of the commissioners King Charles II had sent to look into the affairs of the colony. After listening to their story, Cartwright persuaded the two men to return with him to England to seek backers for their proposed fur trading venture to Hudson Bay.

Cartwright introduced the two adventurers to Sir George Carteret, the richest man in England, who took the two Frenchmen under his wing. Carteret introduced them to King Charles II who was so enthralled with their stories of the Cree and the wealth of furs they harbored that he provided them with lodgings and an allowance until an expedition to Hudson Bay could be organized.

Meanwhile, Carteret organized a group of investors, including Prince Rupert, into a company interested in trading in Hudson Bay. Finally, in 1668 Radisson and Des Groseilliers set out for the Bay in two ships, the Eaglet and the Nonsuch.

The Eaglet, with Radisson on board, was forced back by storms. But the Nonsuch, carrying Des Groseilliers, reached the Bay and returned to England the following year carrying a rich cargo of furs. In this way the theories of Des Groseilliers were finally proved correct.

The following year, in 1670, the Hudson's Bay Company was founded with Radisson and Des Groseilliers as its first employees.

A few years later, the French Minister of Finance, Jean-Baptiste Colbert, persuaded Radisson and Des Groseilliers to return to the service of France. Outfitted with two rundown vessels, they returned to Hudson Bay, where they captured an English ship, the Bachelor's Delight. They brought the seized vessel and its crew to Québec, where the Governor returned it to the English.

In 1684 the famous duo, who had spent so many years together, finally parted ways. Radisson returned to his English wife and to the service of the Hudson's Bay Company. Médard Chouart, Sieur Des Groseilliers – after many frequent and long absences – went back to his wife and children in Trois Rivières, where he remained until his death in 1696. Pierre Esprit Radisson died in London in 1710.

The Hudson's Bay Company, which owes so much of its early success to the endeavors of the two adventurers, is still operating today, though as a department store chain, no longer in the fur trading business. However, you can still purchase one of its famous woolen blankets, though with dollars instead of beaver pelts. At one time it controlled almost a third of what is today Canada. In 1870, three years after Confederation, the government of Canada acquired the land, called Rupert's Land, from the Company for 1.5 million dollars.

Afterword

Thank you for reading Beaver Coats And Guns. For more background information about this book, please visit:

http://beavercoatsandguns.com

Richard Lapointe
December, 2016

CPSIA information can be obtained
at www.ICGtesting.com
Printed in the USA
LVOW13s1443150217
524370LV00027B/597/P